Love Me Even When It Hurts

Jelissa

Lock Down Publications and Ca$h
Presents

Love Me Even When It Hurts
A Novel by *Jelissa*

Jelissa

Lock Down Publications
P.O. Box 870494
Mesquite, Tx 75187

Visit our website @
www.lockdownpublications.com

Copyright 2018 Love Me Even When It Hurts

First Edition November 2018
Printed in the United States of America

This is a work of fiction. Names, characters, places, and incidents either are products of the author's imagination or are used fictitiously. Any similarity to actual events or locales or persons, living or dead, is entirely coincidental.

Lock Down Publications
Like our page on Facebook: Lock Down Publications @
www.facebook.com/lockdownpublications.ldp
Cover design and layout by: **Dynasty Cover Me**
Book interior design by: **Shawn Walker**
Edited by: **Lauren Burton**

Stay Connected with Us!

Text **LOCKDOWN** to 22828 to stay up-to-date with new releases, sneak peaks, contests and more...
Or **CLICK HERE** to sign up.
Thank you.

Like our page on Facebook:

Lock Down Publications: Facebook

Join Lock Down Publications/The New Era Reading Group

Visit our website @
www.lockdownpublications.com

Follow us on Instagram:

Lock Down Publications: Instagram

Email Us: We want to hear from you!

Submission Guideline.

Submit the first three chapters of your completed manuscript to ldpsubmissions@gmail.com, subject line: Your book's title. The manuscript must be in a .doc file and sent as an attachment. Document should be in Times New Roman, double spaced and in size 12 font. Also, provide your synopsis and full contact information. If sending multiple submissions, they must each be in a separate email.

Have a story but no way to send it electronically? You can still submit to LDP/Ca$h Presents. Send in the first three chapters, written or typed, of your completed manuscript to:

LDP: Submissions Dept
Po Box 870494
Mesquite, Tx 75187

DO NOT send original manuscript. Must be a duplicate.

Provide your synopsis and a cover letter containing your full contact information.

Thanks for considering LDP and Ca$h Presents.

Dedication

To the greatest man I know, I love you with everything that I am. I thank God for you. For the wonderful man that you are. Your encouragement and desire to see me push further in my writing career has been my driving force. Thank you for seeing in me what every other man has failed to see. You've loved me at my worst and loved me at my best. I'm forever yours.

To my baby boys RayJ & AJ, mommy loves you. Everything I do is for you two. Thank you for being the greatest sons ever! Mommy loves you with all her heart.

Jelissa

Chapter 1

Sharome "Rome" Mills

Five degrees below zero. The wind blew harshly through the night, causing the snow to crash into my skin, making it freeze. My hot breath made it seem as if I was exhaling some sort of smoke from my lungs, but it was simply too cold for me to be outside. My toes were frozen, and so were my fingers and the tip of my nose. I had been beating on the back door of my mother's house for over ten minutes and had gotten no response. The only reason I didn't leave was because I knew she was inside, but just ignoring me. I was more than familiar with this routine.

I pounded on the door again, this time harder than before, and suddenly the back light that illuminated the door came on and I could hear the two-by-four being removed from across the door on the other side. I took a step back and blew into my frozen hands, trying to find some sort of relief from the pain of the cold. The thin jacket I'd managed to grab before I was forced into the night by my mother, did little to protect me. I was shaking worse than a child afraid of a monster.

The door opened, and my mother stepped out into the backyard seconds before my brother followed her outside. Both were bundled up in Gucci leather jackets and thick, heavily insulated gloves.

My mother fixed her earmuffs on her head, then curled her lip up at me. "You beatin' on this here door all hard and shit. Better mean you made your quota for the day, or you already know what's finna happen to yo ass, am I right?"

I hugged my body as the wind seemed to pick up speed and attack me as if it had somethin' against me personally. My teeth chattered, and my knees began to knock. The cold was once again getting the better of me. "I. I. I made eighty dollas. I could have made more than that, but I'm too cold. I can't even think straight," I replied, blowing into my right fist.

My mother shook her head and gave me a look of disgust. "But yo' quota is two hundred dollars, which means you are a hundred and twenty dollas short. So get yo' black ass back out there and make it happen, or else."

She stepped to the side and my brother took two steps in my direction with a mug on his face. He spit into the snow and wiped his mouth with his gloved hand.

I took two steps back. My brother, Kamakazi Mills, was two years older than me and built like a young Mike Tyson. He went by "Kazi". Every time I fucked up, my mother would make him get on my ass, and that fool was relentless. He had a habit of beating me like I was some random nigga on the streets. It's like he had disregarded the fact we had the same blood coursing through our veins. Some days he would fuck me up so bad I'd be bedridden for weeks.

Shit, I was already freezing, and the last thing I wanted to do was get my ass whooped by this nigga. All I wanted to do was get into the house under the heat. After I had warmed up, I'd do whatever my mother wanted me to do in them streets. I understood it was my job to bring in some form of income. I was seventeen now, and before my father had gotten killed the summer before by some of the members from his mob, he'd always said a man became a man at the age of twelve, and from then on he was supposed to support the family by any and every means necessary. I didn't have no problem with that, but tonight it was just too cold outside. I hated the cold and everything that came along with it.

"Look, Ma, I'll come back out here tonight after I warm up a li'l bit. I can't feel none of my limbs, word is bond." I stomped my foot on the pavement to gain feeling back into it, then blew into my fist again.

I took a step to my left, getting ready to go into the house when my mother leaned back and pushed me, sending me stumbling backward. I landed in the snow and could feel it all along the back of my neck. She stood over me with anger in her eyes.

"Nigga, you know the rules. If you ain't got yo' quota, you ain't coming in this house. Yo' punk ass gon' freeze to death. That's how this shit work." She frowned. "Get yo' ass up and get out there and go make that hundred and twenty, then bring yo' stupid-ass back here so you can get some sleep, 'cuz you going to school in the morning. That's for damn sure." She slammed her hands on her hips and jerked her head on her neck. "Well? Get yo' ass up! Now, boy!"

Kazi took it upon himself to reach down and yank me upward, but I was heated, and I wasn't with this fool touching me. As soon as I got to my feet, I pushed the shit out of him after smacking his hands away from me.

"Get yo' hands off me, Kazi. You always trying to act like you her enforcer or somethin'. She 'on't need yo' help." I dusted the snow off me while at the same time mugging him. What I really wanted to say would have gotten me royally screwed over, and I probably would have never been able to get back into the house that night. Or at all, for that matter.

Smack!

My mother walked up on me fast, raised her hand, and smacked the hell out of me before pushing me back down. "Don't put yo' hands on my son. You not his daddy. I run this shit." She walked over to my brother and looked him over closely. "You know what you gotta do, right, baby?"

He slung his hands downward with so much force, unleashing those deadly weapons I'd watched him batter niggaz all up and down the streets of Newark, New Jersey with. I already knew what was finna go down. Even though I knew I couldn't fuck with his bidness, I wasn't about to let him just bang me this night. I was gon' fight him back as best I could.

He took his Gucci leather coat off and dropped it to the snow, threw up his guards, and rolled his head around on his neck as if he was a boxer. "Mama, go stand yo' ass over there. I'm about to whoop this nigga and melt this snow with his blood. Don't break this shit up, either, or else me and you gon' have some problems. You understand that?" he asked, looking over his shoulders at our small mother.

She swallowed and backed away toward the house with her eyes wide open. "Yeah, Kazi, I hear you. But baby, please don't hurt him too bad. Don't send that boy back to the hospital. The last time you did that, I had them people all in my business for a month straight. We don't have time for that right now. It's already too much shit going on." Smoke from the freezing air rose from her mouth. Her light-skinned cheeks were red, along with her nose.

Kazi grunted, then spit into the snow. "I got this. I'm the man of the house now, so I know how to discipline this li'l nigga." He turned to me with an evil scowl on his face. "You already know what time it is, money. Word is bond, I'm finna get all up in that ass."

I blew hot air into both of my hands as my brother bounced on his toes for a second, then started in my direction with his closed fists guarding his face. I felt my heart pounding in my chest. My head was spinning, and I felt lighter on my feet the closer he got to me. As soon as he was in arm's reach, he jabbed me straight in the jaw, knocking me backward. *Bam!*

I tried to keep my footing, but the snow was so heavy in our backyard that I wound up tripping and falling hard on my ass with my face stinging worse than ever.

"Get yo' punk-ass up, Rome. You think you running shit, nigga? I'm 'bout to put my foot all up in yo' ass." He took three steps forward and stepped into the heavy snow as the wind blew hard across the night. As soon as he was close enough to me, he reached down and yanked me up, raised his fist, and punched me square in the nose, busting it. Then he picked me up and slammed me by my neck into the snow bank. *Whoom!*

The impact caused me to lose my breath. I hollered out in pain, then turned onto my side as I felt the blood coursing out of my nostrils. Sharp pains shot up and down my spine, ending at my toes. I groaned as I wallowed in agony.

"Get up, li'l nigga. Get yo' ass up and fight me, or I'm finna kill yo' ass right here in front of our mother." He stomped through the snow and attempted to pick me up. My neck jerked around loosely on my shoulders as I felt him lifting me into the air and slamming me down with so much velocity I bounced up from the snow only to land right back on it.

I closed my eyes as pain shot from everywhere. I could never understand why my brother did me like this, why he hated me so much and insisted on causing me so much pain. Another thing I couldn't understand was why I loved him so much and why trying to hurt him before this night had never crossed my mind. I just couldn't imagine shedding his blood, which was ultimately my own.

"Kazi, come on, baby. He's had enough. Let him up so he can go and make that hundred and twenty he owes for his quota. You ain't got nothin' else to prove to mama, baby."

While she was saying this, he had straddled me with his hand around my neck, I assumed getting ready to choke me out. But after my mother said those words, he looked over his shoulder at her and curled his upper lip. "Didn't I tell yo' ass I had this right here, huh? Ain't I the muthafuckin' man of the house? Don't I take care of all of us? Huh?" He threw me down, stood up, and made his way across the snow toward her while I tried to gather myself.

The snow started coming down in big blankets, making it impossible to see and breathe. I struggled to sit up. By the time I did, I saw Kazi grab our mother by the throat with one hand and slam her against the back of our house before leaning his face forward into hers. "Answer me, Mama. I ain't gon' ask you again."

She stood on her tippy-toes to take away some of the pressure he was applying to her neck. "Yes, baby! Ack! Ack! I'm sorry. I'm sorry, baby. Please don't hurt me."

13

Jelissa

He must've tightened his grip because the next thing I heard was the sound of her choking and gagging for air.

"I told you, let me handle my bidness. You stay in a woman's place. I'm the man of the house now that my old man dead and gone. I'm the new him. Got me, li'l lady?"

She nodded her head. He threw her more violently into the back of the house, causing her to slowly slide down to the ground until she was sitting Indian-style in the snow, holding her neck and gasping for air.

He turned his sights back to me. I was standing on my feet with my fists balled as hard as I could make them. I didn't know what I was about to do, but I knew for sure I wasn't finna sit by and just let him put his hands on our mother, regardless of how she treated me.

He walked up on me with a sneer on his face, and as soon as he got close enough, I swung as hard as I could and hit him with a right hook that sounded like somebody had clapped their hands together. My fist crashed into his jaw, catching him off guard. He spit into the air, then fell in slow motion to the snow with his hands out in front of him to avoid the worst possible impact.

"I'm ti'ed of yo' shit, Kazi. I'm ti'ed of you puttin' yo' hands on our mother. Nigga, if you gon' kill me, then come on. Because I ain't goin' no more. Word is bond." I cocked my leg back and kicked him straight in the ribs, flipping him on his back.

He groaned out in pain, then started to get up. I stepped back to gather myself. I looked up and to my left, seeing our next-door neighbor's bedroom light pop on. A'Leeseea's face appeared in the window, watching the whole scene unfold. For some reason just knowing she was watching gave me a sense of false courage. I say false because I already knew Kazi was getting ready to whoop my ass in the worst way. I was secretly hoping it stopped at the ass whoopin' and he didn't flat-out kill me.

Before I could even make sense of what I'd just done, I threw up my guards and bum-rushed him, throwing one blow after the next, trying to connect with his face in any way I could. The first blow he blocked. The second one

14

caught him in the lip and busted it. The third he slapped away, then he took my wrist and pulled me into him, punched me in the face before flipping me over his back and straddling me. I struggled to get up, but this nigga lifted weights every single day. It felt like I was being held down by a semi-truck. He had his knees on my wrists and his left hand around my throat.

"You bitch-ass nigga! I'm finna kill you!" He slapped me, then delivered three punches to my face.

My blood spurted across the snow, and I started to see stars. It was this night that told me I had to step my boxing game all the way up. This fool was manhandling me, and I wasn't cool with it in the least bit. I didn't care if he was my brother or not.

I could feel the blood all over me as I saw his fist raise only to come down once again, hitting me in the right eye, blackening it.

"I told you, nigga. I run this shit now. I'm the king. You dare raise yo' hand to me?" He reached into his waistband and pulled out his .45 so fast it was like a blur. The next thing I knew it was pressed up against my forehead. "Yo, moms. Word is bond, I'm finna kill this nigga. Tell 'em you love him before I blow his brains out across backyard, no-mercy style." He spit into my face, tightening his grip on my neck.

"No!" Our mother screamed. "Please don't do it, Kazi. It's not that serious, baby. You run this family. You in charge now. Ain't nobody contesting that."

Kazi shook his head as the wind's speed picked up once again, freezing me to my very core. I could feel my face sticky with my own blood. I felt helpless and weaker than I'd ever felt before. I was tired of being on the receiving end of my brother's wrath, tired of being treated less than human by my own family. And as much as I loved my mother, she was included in that statement.

"Nah, Ma. I gotta splash this nigga. I ain't gon' feel shit for 'im, nah mean? Just gon' chalk this one up to a deadly sibling rivalry. I ain't trying to share you wit' nobody anyway, Ma. Period. Fuck this nigga." He lowered

Jelissa

his eyes into slits and cocked the hammer on his .45, pressing it so hard into my forehead it felt like he'd already pulled the trigger. "Tell me why I shouldn't smoke yo' punk ass in front of *my* mother?" he growled, spitting in my face in the process.

"Because if you pull that trigger, I'ma have yo' ass booked into Newark County Jail on the charge of first degree intentional homicide, *after* I pump one of these hot muthafuckas in yo' ass so you can see what it feel like," Idris said before cocking a big-ass shotgun. "Get yo' ass off of him and toss that gun over here by me. Yo' father probably turning over in his grave right now."

Kazi jumped off of me with his eyes bucked. He took the gun and tossed it over by the foot of our neighbor, Idris. "Say, Shotgun, it ain't even like that. I was just fucking around with the li'l nigga because he so soft. I wasn't finna kill him or nothin'. That's my word." He tried to laugh, then curled his upper lip.

I knew he hated Idris. The police officer was all he or any of his friends could talk about behind closed doors. They all called Idris dirty and said he was a lunatic with a badge. The man had once been plugged on the mean streets of Bergen. Back in the day he ran with a group of killas that called themselves the Shotgun Posse. Out of the ten of them, Idris was the only one still alive. The other nine were dead and gone and had suffered terrible deaths by the streets.

Idris leaned over and put the .45 Kazi had tossed to him on his waist, then held the shotgun at eye level, aiming it directly at Kazi. "I don't like how you get down in front of yo' mama, li'l nigga. You disrespectful, and you think you runnin' shit out here in these streets when in actuality you ain't nothing but a parasite I don't mind stepping on." He turned to look at our mother. "Shavon, you good? Are you hurt in any way?"

She stood up and stumbled on her feet before catching her balance. She looked over at Idris and frowned. "What the fuck are you doing in my yard, Shotgun? This ain't got nothin' to do wit' you. This is family bidness." She

16

scrunched her nose and looked at him as if she wanted to kill him.

He smiled and turned his head to the side. "Aw, I see you still harboring ill feelings toward me, huh? Ain't that somethin'?" He looked over to me. "You can't keep letting them do this shit to you, Rome. You need to ask yo' mother why she hate you so much. Why she be letting this nigga right here do whatever he wanna do to you?" He looked over to her and shook his head. "Shavon, you need to let that old shit go. Had I not broke this up tonight, you would've had one son in the county and one in the morgue. You need to get yo' family in order, and I'm willing to help you if I can."

My mother ran up on him and moved his shotgun out of the way. "I'd rather die before I let you help me with anything. I hate yo' fucking guts," she spat with tears running down her cheeks.

He looked at her for a long time as the snow continued to come down harder from the sky. I could feel blood dripping off my chin, and it seemed every part of my body hurt. I was frozen and yearned to be in a warm house. At the same time, I was feeling as if I could kill Kazi. I was done taking the abuse from him and really wondered if he would have killed me had Idris not shown up to the party.

Idris, in one swift motion, snatched her and planted her against the house with one hand while he held out the shotgun in his other, aimed at Kazi. "Anybody move, they catching a slug. And trust me, my word is most definitely my bond, kid."

Once he saw we were unmoving, he looked down at my mother. An evil smile came across his face. "You still can't let the past go, huh? Still hanging onto old shit you really don't know nothing about?" He sucked his teeth and slowly shook his head while holding her more firmly against the back of the house.

"Fuck you, Shotgun. You ain't shit to me. I know you a snake, nigga. You ain't got me fooled. You can wear the biggest badge in the world, but I know who the real man is underneath it all, and I hate yo' fuckin' guts!" my

17

mother hollered through clenched teeth. She struggled against him to try to break free.

I balanced myself on my feet and made my way over to them blood still dripping from my lip. I felt dizzy and like one of my ribs may have been broken. It hurt whenever I took a breath. "Shotgun, let my moms go, man. Please. Let me take her in the house where it's warm."

He continued to look down at her with a menacing look on his face. Then he glanced back over his shoulder at me. "Yeah, you do that, Rome. You take yo' moms in the house, but one day you ask her why she hate you so much, why she love inflicting pain on you both physically and mentally." He leaned forward and kissed her on the cheek and she cringed, still struggling against him. "You take care of yourself, Shavon, and grow up. Let the past be the past. Don't make this boy pay for it."

He released her and laid his shotgun against his right shoulder, then glanced upward to the back of his house next door. As soon as he did, I noted that Leesee's light went off in her room and the curtains were moved back into place.

He mugged the shit out of Kazi and sucked his teeth once again real loudly. "Karma is a bitch, Kazi. One day you gon' see that to be true. That li'l nigga right there ain't always gon' bow down to you. One day you gon' be the prey and he's going to be the predator with no mercy. Mark my words."

He hopped over the gate and disappeared into his back door after saluting us.

Chapter 2

A'Leeseea "Leesee" Evans

My heart damn near skipped a beat when I saw my mother's fiancé, Idris, look up at my window and right into my eyes, it seemed, as I watched the events of my next-door neighbors. They were always shittin' on Rome. Either the older brother, Kazi, was beatin' him up in front of everybody or his crazy-ass momma was locking him out of the house and forcing him to sleep in the backyard.

I thanked the Lord my parents weren't that bad as I fixed my curtain and sat on the edge of my bed, setting the alarm on my phone to go off at 5:30 in the morning. I slid under the covers and said a silent prayer for Rome. I prayed for his peace and asked our Father in Heaven to watch over him through the night and into the morning. I didn't know what his mother and brother had in store for him that night, so I could only ask God for His ultimate protection. As soon as I finished, I crossed myself with the crucifix and turned onto my side and closed my eyes.

Just as I was about to doze off, I heard a faint knocking on my bedroom door, and then it opened. *Not this shit again.* In stepped Idris. He crept over to the bed and sat down on the edge, extending his hand onto my hip before caressing it. My eyes popped open. *Why won't this nigga leave me alone?*

"Baby girl? Baby girl? Are you awake?" he whispered only loud enough for me to hear him.

I tried my best to fake being asleep. I didn't feel like dealing with him tonight. I was tired and had a whole week of exams at school. I needed my rest.

I continue to ignore him, so he took it upon himself to slide into the bed behind me in a spooning fashion. I felt him lean in and begin to suck on the back of my neck, using first his lips, then his teeth ever so lightly. I felt the tingles go down my spine, causing me to shudder. I tried my best to not allow this shit to get to me, but this older

Jelissa

man was something else when it came my body. He had more control over it than I did. When he sucked on my neck a little harder and pulled me back into him until my butt was pressed up against his dick, I couldn't help but moan. Man, why didn't my pussy do what my mind told it to? She always betrayed me when it came down to Idris.

"What do you want, Idris? You betta stop before my mother wake up and catch you," I whimpered as I felt him slide the cover down, creep inside, then pull it back over us. The feel of his muscular chest against my back, his hot breath tickling the hairs on my neck, and his penis pushing on my ass like a probe was enough to wet my panties.

He reached around, cupped my left breast, and squeezed it ever so tenderly, trapping the nipple that poked through the fabric of my gown with his two fingers and pulling it, sucking on my neck again. "I need some of you, baby girl. I gotta have some of my baby. It's been a long day. I been through a lot. Come on, baby, give Daddy what he needs."

My thighs opened to his touch. He straddled me and flipped me onto my back, pulling my nightgown all the way up before ripping my panties from between my legs and throwing them to the floor. Then he slid down my body until his face was between my legs. He pushed my knees to my chest and slurped my throbbing pussy into his mouth loudly, causing me to let out a loud, breathless moan. I grabbed one of my pillows to the right of me and bit down on it to muffle my screams as I felt him separate my sex lips and trap my clitoris with thick lips, running his hot, wet, slippery tongue back and forth across the bundle of nerves, drawing out my little cries of pleasure.

"I love the taste of you, baby girl. This my pussy right here. This belong to Daddy. You belong to me. You hear me?" He sucked my sex lips back into his mouth and worked me over like a professional.

My head shook from side to side. As much as I wanted to fight against him, I had not one ounce of fight in me. I screamed into the pillow and tried to keep from releasing my juices onto his face, but I couldn't help it.

Love Me Even When It Hurts

Damn, that tongue. His tongue continued to attack the hot nub of my clitoris as he sucked on it with so much force. He slid two fingers deep into my center and began to run them in and out.

With my knees to my chest, I felt trapped and vulnerable. As crazy as it sounds, it only added to my pleasure. I felt myself cumming hard, bucking up from the bed, nearly sittin' up just to fall back down while my teeth bit into the pillow, screaming deep within my throat. And then it happened. I came so hard I felt like I was having a seizure and couldn't stop shaking, but that didn't stop him and his assault on my clit. He kept on licking, sucking, and nipping at it with his teeth, demanding my pussy leak for him again.

He straddled me again, placing my right ankle onto his shoulder, and slid his big, thick dick into me slowly, plunging deeply.

"Uh! Idris, no. We can't. Please, my mother gon' catch us. Please, just –"

He placed his big hand over my mouth and started to stroke me faster and deeper, again and again, making sure my juices coated every inch of his dick. All 10½ inches of it. Every time he slammed forward, it caused my eyes to roll into the back of my head, and a jolt of pleasure shot through me like electricity. A jolt of electricity I couldn't control. *Damn. This. Dick.* I hated how much my pussy reacted to him. To his touch.

"You. My. Baby. Girl. Leesee. Do. You. Hear. Me?" he asked, strokin' me so fast I could barely concentrate. I closed my eyes tight, reached up, and dug my nails into his waist as he attacked me like a savage. "I. Love. You. Baby. Girl."

Faster and faster he plunged, going deeper into my body. I felt his hand grip my right breast and squeeze. He went back and forth between both breasts, sucking, licking, and pinching the nipples while his dick darted in and out of me until he was coming deep within my channel, grunting into my ear before collapsing on top of me.

Jelissa

The next morning Idris woke me up five minutes before my alarm went off with a tray of breakfast. He slid onto my bed and kissed me on the forehead, causing me to open my eyes.

"Good morning, baby girl. Rise and shine. It's time to get up and go kill them exams," he said, smiling at me with that handsome face.

My mother stuck her head into my doorway with a toothbrush already in her mouth. "Idris, leave that girl alone and come in here and finish cooking breakfast for everybody else. Nia hungry, too. I told you, you can't be having no favorites. You gotta love both of my daughters the same." She rolled her eyes and left out of the doorway.

"If you take yo' ass into the kitchen, you'll see I already fixed her breakfast, and yours, too. Don't get up wit' all that bullshit. It's too early. I'm just trying to make sure my baby girl greet the morning in a positive state of mind because she gotta handle them exams today, especially if she trying to get into NYU, thank you very much." He shook his head, then looked down on me as I yawned with a smile on his face. "How do you feel, baby girl?"

I sat all the way up and tried to put a smile on my face as well, though I was feeling a little smothered. I didn't like when he was home because I had no privacy. I didn't like how he invaded my personal space, and my mother seemed oblivious to what was going on between us right behind her back. I felt dirty and so alone.

"I feel okay. I wish you wouldn't have woken me up like that last night, 'cuz now I'm tired. And besides, I thought we weren't going to do that anymore. You promised," I said, barely above a whisper. I knew Idris had a horrible temper. The last thing I wanted was to piss him off. I knew he would have no problem beating my ass, even if it was just with his hand. Him chastising me like that always turned him on, which is how things had started sexually between us to begin with.

Love Me Even When It Hurts

He took the fork and scooped up some of the cheese omelet and held it out to me. "Huh, baby, eat up and get your strength."

I opened my mouth reluctantly and ate the eggs he was offering.

"I told you before that you're my baby girl now. That you belong to me. If I wanna climb in bed with you every single night, then that's just what I'ma do, because you are mine. Now, tell me you belong to me. Tell me I'm daddy. Hurry up, because I need to hear it." He reached over and put his hand around my neck as if he were preparing to choke me. "Tell me, Leesee. I need to hear you say it." He demanded through gritted teeth, applying pressure to my neck.

My heart began to pound in my chest. "I belong to you, Idris. I belong to you," I complied, my eyes watering.

He shook his head, looked over his shoulder out toward the hallway. "Nah, fuck that 'Idris' shit. Call me Daddy. You my baby girl. That's what I mean. So, tell Daddy you belong to him and only him. Tell me!" he growled through clenched teeth.

The pressure of his hand around my neck increased. I prayed my mother would walk up on him and kick him out of the house. I blinked as the tears glided down my cheeks. "I belong to you, Daddy. I'm your baby girl. Now please, let my neck go."

He leaned forward and kissed me on the lips, sucking them into his mouth before grabbing the bottom of my chin roughly. "Kiss me, Leesee. I need you."

I started to kiss him back as he sat the tray on the lamp stand and pulled me more into his embrace, kissing me passionately, then licking my tears from my cheeks. "I love you, Leesee. I been loving you ever since you came into this world. You belong to me, and I'll kill a muthafucka over you wit' no hesitation. Play wit' me and find out. Betta not nobody lay their finger on my baby girl. I'll kill they whole family. That's my word. Yo' daddy owed me his life, and he gave me you. And I ain't giving you up. You hear me?"

Jelissa

I nodded as he licked away my tears. "Yes, Idris, I hear you."

He lifted his head and eyed me closely. "And no more of that 'Idris' shit. From now on you call me daddy, and only daddy. I love you, baby. I swear I love you so much. When you get out of school today, I'ma take you on a little shopping spree. Only the best for my li'l girl."

Ninety minutes later, I sat with my head down behind the wheel of my Jeep Grand Cherokee, tired of the shit I'd been going through with this man. I was missing my *real* father, who was locked away out in New York with a life sentence for murder. I felt so trapped. I just needed to talk to him so I could tell him what I was going on with my mother's boyfriend, or whoever the fuck he was to her. For all the dick I was getting, anyone would have thought he was my man.

He was more than familiar with Idris. He called him Shotgun, and on more than one occasion he told me back in the day they were old enemies. He, my mother, and Shotgun all attended the same high school and were raised in the same projects. My mother dated them both at the same time, and I was born during her sophomore year, and it was then she had crossed completely over to my father so they could do the best they could for me as parents.

After high school, my father stayed in the streets and Idris wound up going into the police academy. A few years later my father caught a homicide to an officer and was sentenced to life in prison without the possibility of parole, though he swore on my life he was innocent and was set up.

My dad wasn't away for more than a year before Idris was knocking on our door. A month later he'd fully moved in, and my mother became pregnant again with my little sister, Nia. She was Idris' daughter, though he appeared to give me more love and affection than he did her for some reason. By the age of fifteen, I was the object of his sexual fascination, and sixteen was when he started to act on his sexual fascinations with groping, fondling, and nonstop touching.

24

Love Me Even When It Hurts

Nia opened my passenger door and slid into the seat, taking her Gucci handbag and setting it on her lap. "What's the matter with you?" she asked, pulling down the sun visor so she could see her reflection in the mirror. She cheesed her teeth, then ran her finger across them.

I started the Jeep, then pulled away from the curb. "Nothin'. I'm just a little tired. I didn't get enough sleep, and now I got these damn tests all day." I yawned and shook my head. "It ain't enough time in a day."

She snickered. "Yeah, I bet. You can't be having dudes jump through your window at night, grinding all in that pussy, then acting like you regret it come the morning. Shid, if you can't handle it, then next time come and knock on my door. I'm fiending for some." She pushed the sun visor back up and sat back in her seat, plugging her cell phone into car jack and scrolling down her music log as the sun shone through the window, illuminating the snow as it fell from the sky. She crossed her thick thighs, causing her Prada skirt to rise on her brown skin. "So, who was it?"

I jerked my head back and looked over to her with a worried look on my face. "Who was who?"

She sucked her teeth loudly, then gave me a smirk. "You know what I'm askin' you. Who was it in your bedroom last night at about two in the morning? I heard you moaning and your headboard knocking into the wall. So either you had somebody in there, or you were working yourself over pretty good. Either way, you're about to tell me something, cuz it ain't the first time I heard you gettin' down in the middle of the night. Geez, your noises drive me crazy," she said, setting the music so SZA came out of my speakers.

Me and my sister Nia looked like brown-skinned, Asian-eyed twins. We were both slim up top and thick down low. She was just a little taller than me, maybe about five feet, five inches, whereas I was five feet, four inches tall. Our hair hung a little past our shoulders, naturally curly, and the only major physical difference between us was the prominent mole on the left side of my upper lip.

"Let's just say I had a real freaky dream I couldn't get off my mind until I got it out of me. Okay? Now, let's leave it at that." I replied, praying we could change the subject. I didn't know what my sister would do or think if she knew I was sleeping wit' her father. She would probably hate me and never speak to me again, and in a world so cold, my sister was all I had. I would do anything for her, and vice versa.

She reached into her Gucci bag and pulled out a small bottle of lotion, squirting a tad bit into the palm of her right hand, then rubbing it into her kneecaps. "Have we gotten to a place where you can't keep it real with me anymore? Huh?" she asked without looking over to me.

That made the hair stand on my skin. I was hoping she wasn't saying she knew who was in my room last night. My throat became dry, making it hard for me to swallow. "What are you talking about?" I looked over to her, at the same time pulling into our school's parking lot. There were kids rolling up in all kinds of expensive cars with their music blaring. The snow continue to fall in heavily.

Nia squirted more lotion into her hand, then started to massage it into her thighs, causing her skirt to rise higher and higher. I was wondering why she hadn't already done that at home, but then remembered just how dry our skin got in the wintertime. We needed extra coats. Luckily for me, I was wearing Prada jeans, so I was good, though under them I knew I was probably ashy as hell.

She smiled. "Nah, I'm just saying I did open your door a little bit, and I saw you rolled into a ball while some nigga was beatin' yo' back in. I was about to come all the way in your room and tell you to share his ass, but then I heard our mother's door open. And being the *good sister* I am, I went and caused a distraction for you while you did your thing, so I'd say you owe me more than the lies you feeding me right now." She pulled down her skirt and sprayed her Kim K perfume into her cleavage.

Love Me Even When It Hurts

I lowered my head. I didn't like lying to my sister, or anybody for that matter. I was on the verge of telling her what was really good when her boyfriend, Jamal, walked up to my truck and opened the passenger door with a rose in his hand. "Yo, Nia, I'm tryna kiss them lips before homeroom, ma, word is bond. I been thinking about yo' li'l sexy ass all night. Them flicks you sent was hot, baby. What's good?"

He leaned into the truck and a big wave of cold air rushed inside, freezing me. The next thing I knew they were tonguing each other down while my sister moaned deep within her throat, opening her legs for his hand to invade her special place.

I covered my eyes. "Look, Nia, lock up my truck when y'all done, and don't be late. I'm finna go inside." I grabbed my Hermes handbag from the backseat, along with my laptop and book bag.

Nia moaned. "Look, sis, I need some dick. Let us handle our handle real fast, then I swear I'll be right in. Come on, baby, open that back door and give me a quickie," she moaned, out of breath while his hand continued to manipulate her between her legs.

"Nah, come get in my Navigator. It's more room. I need to hit that shit right. All I need is fifteen minutes."

That was the last thing I heard before I walked away from them and headed into the school building with the wind blowing at my back.

Jelissa

Chapter 3

Rome

The next morning after my brother called himself getting ready to kill me, I was awakened by a light tapping on my cheek with a .9 millimeter. Upon opening my eyes, he pointed the gun at my forehead. "Bitch-nigga, Mama say it's time for you to earn some real bread, so you gon' roll wit' me today, and we gon' get you situated in one of my 'bandos. That li'l punk-ass two hunnit she askin' of you ain't no real nigga money. That shit is insulting of our Queen to ask for you to provide. Nigga, if you ain't bringin' in at least two gees a day, then you ain't on shit. So get yo' li'l ass up and let's get a move on. Time is money, and you ain't got neither."

I jumped up, went into the bathroom after grabbing me a nice Tom Ford fit, closing the bathroom door and ran the shower water. I stripped down and looked myself over in the full-length mirror on the back of the door. My ribs were killing me. I lifted my arm into the air and ran my right hand up and down my left side to try to see if there were any bones protruding out anywhere. Thankfully there weren't, even though my whole left side was a shade of crimson. I took a deep breath and looked at myself in the mirror. My right eye looked a little swollen, and the area under it was a shade of purple. My yellow skin looked dry, and I was in desperate need of a good shower.

I watched my gray eyes look back at me, and for some reason I just felt lower than scum. I felt worthless, like the air in my body was pointless. It had been so long since I had received any form of love from anybody, and I think it was beginning to take a toll on me. I was finding it harder and harder to look forward to the next day. On most nights I prayed I didn't even wake up. Shit, I didn't feel like there was any reason to. I loved both my mother and brother so much, and I just wished they cared about me even half as much as I did them. I was so broken, just yearning for somebody to truly love me.

I flexed in the mirror and watched my abs tighten. My stomach was nice cut up for a seventeen year old. My chest developed like a man who had been lifting weights his whole life, though all I did was about a hundred push-ups every morning.

I couldn't help hating the reflection I saw in the mirror. I hated myself because the woman who had given birth to me hated me so much, and I didn't know why. I wanted to ask her so bad, wanted to ask her what it was Idris was talking about. I was wondering if he had the answers to the questions I'd had my whole life.

Kazi beat on the door, scaring the shit out of me and knocking me out of my zone. "Man, hurry yo' ass up. I told you time was money. Nigga, let's go!" he yelled.

I dropped down and did a hundred push-ups, before jumping in the shower for about ten minutes, getting out, and brushing my deep, natural waves. I prayed today would be a good day. I prayed that before it ended, I would have found some reason to wake up the next day.

Twenty minutes later, my brother pulled away from the curb in his money-green Ford Expedition with Kodak Black banging through his speakers. "Yo, I'm tellin' you right now, li'l nigga, I ain't about to coddle you in these streets. I don't know why Moms think I can save yo' ass, but nonetheless, here we are." He took a blunt out of his ashtray and lit the tip, making a right at the stoplight, then stepping on the gas. Smoke filled the car almost immediately.

I let my seat back a li'l bit. "Bruh, I know you older than me and everything, but you ain't gotta talk to me like I'm one of these soft li'l niggas in the streets. I'm still a man, no matter how you feel about me." I was tired of Kazi always trying to downplay me and treat me like I was some random nigga on the street. I had never let nobody other than him punk me, and the only reason I allowed shit to slide with him was cuz I respected and loved him. I knew I wasn't supposed to raise a hand to him, but

Love Me Even When It Hurts

I'd had enough. But there I was, feeling guilty about our fight the previous night. His eye was still a li'l red.

"A man? Nigga, did you just say you a fuckin' man?" He laughed and took a deep pull from his blunt, inhaling the smoke before blowing it into my face.

My upper lip curled up and I felt myself getting heated. I felt like once again he was trying to treat me like a chump. That was getting old to me. "Bruh, why you just can't respect me and love me like yo' li'l brother? You the only dude I know who treat his li'l brother the way you do. That shit ain't cool. One day you gon' need me for somethin', trust me." He handed me the blunt and I took it, taking a deep pull off it, feeling the smoke burn my chest almost immediately.

"Nigga, I don't respect you because you broke. Don't no broke-ass nigga deserve my respect. I don't give a fuck if you my brother or not. That's fuck-shit to me. Then, on top of that, I don't think you about that life like me. Nigga, we got the same blood, same parents and everything, and you somehow came out soft as hell. How many bodies you got under your belt?" he asked, looking me over closely with a scowl on his face.

I squinted my eyes. "Bodies? What you talking about?" I was confused as hell.

He shook his head. "Exactly what the fuck I'm talking about. Murders, nigga! How many muthafuckas you done put in the morgue by use of this steel that's under my seat, locked and loaded?"

I bugged my eyes out of my head. "None. I ain't never had a reason to kill nobody before. But that don't mean I wouldn't if I had to," I retorted, not really knowing if I meant it. To me it took a lot of guts to kill somebody. The act itself was already beasty, but then a person had to worry about the aftermath. Things like being haunted by their spirits, bad dreams, and wondering when the gun was gon' come back on you to take your life. My old man had always said if a nigga lived by the gun, he would eventually die by it. And I believed that shit to be true.

Jelissa

He yanked the blunt out of my hand and took a strong pull from it. "Sometimes you don't need a reason to take yo' anger out on a muthafucka. I just don't like niggaz, period. I'm a lone wolf. I gotta be the leader at all times, and if I feel like a fuck-nigga's a threat to me or what I'm tryna do, I'll clap his ass with no remorse. I'm nineteen with twelve bodies under my belt, and before the winter ends I'm looking to be at twenty, 'cuz it's real out here in these streets. Word is bond. This *my* jungle. *I'm* king 'round dis bitch, feel me?." He curled his lip, reached under his seat, and came up with a .38 special. "Huh," he handed me the gun, "this bitch got six bullets in the chamber. Today, after I break this game down to you a li'l bit, we finna go holler at some of my foes. One nigga in particular I want you to get. You can't begin to understand this game and all that comes along wit' it until you catch yo' first body. After that shit is out the way, you need some pussy from a real thick, older bitch that ain't gon' play wit' you, then we get money." He took another pull from the blunt. "Yo' heart gotta be cold, Rome. You can't give a fuck. Any trace of weaknesses in these streets'll get yo' ass kilt quick. Since Mama asking me to take you under my wing, we gon' do shit my way. Period. You don't tell her shit cuz I run that house. Even *she* under me. You got that?" He reached under his seat and sat a Tech .9 on his lap.

I nodded my head. "Yeah, I get it." Those were the words I said, but in my mind I was terrified about catching my first body. I ain't even have beef with nobody. I didn't see a reason to have to kill. But like he said, he was in charge, and I just had to follow his lead.

We pulled up in front of a brown duplex ten minutes later and Kazi parked his truck. In front of the duplex were about ten dudes with ski masks on their faces and leather Marc Jacob coats on their backs. I could tell they were outside hustlin' because even as we pulled up there were other cars stopping in front of the house. As they did, one of the dudes would go up to the car to serve them his work.

32

Love Me Even When It Hurts

Then the car would pull off and another would appear, and the same thing would take place.

"Look, these niggaz all work for me. Get yo' ass out. I'm finna introduce you to my niggaz." He opened his door and stepped out into the snow and I followed suit, closing my door behind me.

To say I was nervous would have been an understatement. These dudes rubbed me the wrong way. We were on Bergen Street. It was known for savages and cold-blooded killas. The whole hood stayed at war wit' niggaz out of New York, Philly, and even D.C.

As we got out of the truck, I noted a few dudes ducked off in the gangway with choopahs in their hands, knelt down with the barrels pointed in our direction. Kazi looked past the crowd of dudes and into the gangway. "Y'all betta lower them arms, cuz. This Kazi, nigga. Fall back!" he hollered, frowning in anger. They nodded their heads and backed away toward the rear of the house.

"You already know my niggaz stay on point, Kazi. Don't take that shit personal," said a masked dude up in the tree right over our heads. I damn near jumped out of my skin because I had missed him. If he wanted to, he could have chopped down me and my brother with no effort. He was holding an AR-15 with a scope on top of it.

Kazi looked up and smiled. "Paper, what it do, fool? What that bread looking like?"

Paper whistled real loud, then made his way out of the tree. As he jumped to the ground, another dude came from the back of the trap house and climbed into the tree where Paper had previously been. Once he got situated, Paper handed him up the AR-15. "Look, them D.C. niggaz been rolling through wetting our traps all day yesterday over some gambling shit I won't get into out here. Long story short, we at war until we knock that fool Pablo head off. Follow me." Before he headed to the house, he looked me up and down. "Who is this li'l nigga?"

Kazi curled his upper lip. "That's my li'l brother, cuz. He good. He fuckin' wit' me today. After I put him up on game, I'ma put him around the corner in that heroin 'bando. My li'l nigga gotta start eating so he can help wit' the bills. Nah mean?"

Paper nodded. "No doubt, son. Ain't no such thing as a free ride in this world. Muthafuckas gotta get off that porch early and make it happen for the fam." He waved us to follow him once again.

We made our way onto the side of the house where I saw there were four dudes in the gangway, heavily armed and with masks on. I could hear their walkie-talkies going off as they kept their attention on the front of the trap. Paper stopped at the back door and beat on it three times, then followed it with two little knocks. It opened up to reveal a big, heavyset dude who looked like he lifted weights every second of every day. He had to be about six feet, six inches tall and every bit of three hunnit pounds of solid muscle. We were ushered in past him, and I was hit with the strong aroma of cooked cocaine. It was so strong I got lightheaded and sick on the stomach.

Once we made it up the back stairs and into the 'bando, I saw there were four round tables in the middle of the living room, and seated at each table were six people chopping chunks of dope from the kilos in the middle of each table. After they chopped off a nice portion, they placed it onto a digital scale, then dropped it into a sandwich bag and tied it into a knot before placing it into a big Ziploc bag directly to the left of each of them. All of them had medical masks on their faces, and from what I could see, there were more females in there than men.

Paper led us through the house after stopping at each table and looking the operation over closely. After pausing for a moment, he'd nod his head, then move to the next table to do the same thing. We wound up at the back of the duplex with him kneeling down in front of a small safe that looked like a mini refrigerator.

"Yo, son, I don't know where you been getting this flake from, but word is bond, the fien's can't get enough of it. Seem like every time we get all this shit bagged up, an hour later I'm selling out and gotta call you for a re-up. I love how you lacing my traps, cuz. Love, fa real," he said, opening the safe and sticking his hand into it, pulling out two large stacks of money that had rubber bands around them. He handed the money up to Kazi, then closed the safe back and stood up, eyeing my brother.

Kazi thumbed through the bread, then nodded his head. "Yeah, no doubt, kid. You know I gotta keep that sauce. I been fucking wit' them niggaz out of VA real tough. They know how to do bidness. Them studs out of New York ain't been fuckin' wit' Jersey on that proper tip, so I had to find other resources, nah mean? But yo, we got an issue, son."

Before I could even understand what was going on, my brother upped a Glock .40, snatched Paper by the throat, and slammed him into the wall, pressing the gun up against his cheek and at the same time kicking the bedroom door shut with his foot. Paper reached up and tried to take his hand away from his throat, but it was no use. He was caught slipping.

"Rome, reach on that nigga waist and take that gun away. Hurry up before he reach for that muthafucka and I gotta splash him before I get the go-ahead from my niggaz up top."

I was so taken off guard that I was frozen in place. I was trying to figure out what the fuck my brother was up to. Then I remembered how many niggaz were outside heavily armed, and I started to think we were going to be killed. I was beyond scared 'cause this was all new to me.

"Hurry up, Rome! Fuck!" Kazi hollered with spittle coming out of his mouth.

I damn near broke my neck to get over to Paper, and began searching him as if I were the police or something. When I felt the two pistols on his waist, I took them off and tried to hand them to Kazi, but he waved me off.

"Nigga, put 'em on yo' waist. This nigga ain't gon' need 'em no more. And quit acting so fucking stupid before I smoke yo' ass, too."

I put the pistols on my waist and took a step back as I heard a bunch of footsteps on the side of the 'bando. My knees were shaking. I didn't wanna die already, at least not like that. I wished I would have taken my ass to school. I was in my last year. I should've been there taking my exams like everybody else. Damn, I felt so stupid.

Kazi frowned and forced the gun harder into Paper's cheek, then with his other hand he pulled out his phone and punched a number. Seconds later he swallowed and began to talk. "I got that project right now. What you want me to do wit' it?" he asked, looking Paper in the eyes. "Uh-huh. Okay. Shit, that works for me. It's fucked up for him, though. A'ight, one." He hung up the phone, took a step back, and aimed his pistol lower.

Boom! Boom!

Paper hollered out at the top of his lungs as Kazi blew his kneecaps away, causing him to fall to the ground on his stomach. "Argh! Argh! What the fuck, Kazi? What the fuck, man?" He tried to hoist himself upward, but Kazi put his Timbs onto his back and forced him back to his stomach.

"Capo wanna see yo' snitching ass at the warehouse, and you already know what that mean. Bitch-nigga, if it was up to me, I'd leave you stanking right here, right now. But that ain't my call. I'm simply the messenger. I'm picking up where my old man left off." He leaned down and snatched the mask off of Paper's head, then grabbed a handful of his long dreads. "Let's go!"

As soon as he said this, the door swung open and what seemed like ten dudes were waiting outside of it with their assault rifles pointed in our direction. They looked in and saw my brother dragging Paper across the floor with blood oozing out of his kneecaps. They were silent, and I just knew they were about to start busting at us. I said a silent prayer under my breath. I passed gas so many times I was afraid I was about to shit on myself.

Kazi picked up his head and looked them over. "Fuck y'all lookin' at? Somebody go pull me a car around so I can put this snitch-nigga in it. Capo say he wanna see him right away. Y'all help me lift this nigga."

My eyes were bucked as I saw the group of dudes step into the room and get to helping my brother carry Paper through the house while he gave them orders of who was supposed to take over the trap now that Paper would no longer be a part of the operations. I really didn't understand until right then just how plugged my brother really was.

Jelissa

Chapter 4

Leesee

I lay my head on the steering wheel of my Jeep, trying to get enough strength to want to go into the house. My mother was still away at work, and even though nearly every single day me and my sister rolled home together, this particular day she caught a ride with Jamal, which left me alone to face the monster of Idris.

There was no part of me that wanted to go into that house. I didn't know what he was going to have up his sleeve, and I just did not feel like enduring it today. I'd been testing all day at school, skipping lunch to catch a quick nap because I was so tired from the lack of sleep from the night before. Now I just wanted to go inside, take a nice bubble bath, and listen to some Jhene Aiko.

I took a deep breath and exhaled slowly, looking up at my mother's home as the snow fell heavily against my windshield. For some reason the house looked as if it was the one from Amityville. I laughed at that and banged my head against the steering wheel, making the horn sound off three times. I took one more deep breath, then grabbed my things and opened my Jeep door.

The wind blew against my face, freezing my nose and taking my breath away at the same time. I was so glad my Ugg boots had done their job the whole day, because I hated when my toes were frozen over. I started to say a silent prayer in my head, asking God to have Idris asleep, worn out from whatever it was he did all day on the force and in the streets. "Please, please, please be tired and asleep. I just wanna rest," I said to myself, walking up the steps.

I missed my father so much. I was thinking about asking my grandmother if she could take me out to see him that weekend. I just needed to be held by a man who actually cared about me. One who didn't look at me as if I were a piece of meat or a little forbidden girl in his

Jelissa

fantasies. I yearned for real love and didn't feel like I'd had any ever since my father was taken away.

I put my key into the lock and turned it. I closed my eyes and took another deep breath before pushing it in, stepping inside. As soon as I got into the small hallway, I nearly jumped out of my skin because there Idris was, right there waiting on me with a bag from Eves St. Laurent and a smaller one from Tiffany.

"Hey, baby girl." He smiled, "I been missing you all day long. I got some things for you that I know you gon' like." He stepped forward and pulled me into his embrace before I could even utter a word. "Yo' mama ain't gon' be home until late. She working a double, and I gave Nia permission to spend some time wit' that li'l boy Jamal, or whatever his name is. So we got enough time for us to do us. Ain't you happy, baby?"

I felt my heart drop and my stomach flip over three times. I felt sick, scared and alone. I thought about running, but it was like he held me more tightly within his embrace as he said the last part. I could hear him sniffing my hair, and that creeped me out. I didn't know why this man desired me so much, why it was he just had to have me. I mean, why me and not my mother? Why would he become engaged to a woman when he only desired her daughter? I asked myself this question time and time again, not knowing my question was honestly the answer.

I don't remember when I'd put my laptop down, along with the rest of my things. What I do remember was him pushing me against the wall face-first, getting behind me, and kicking my legs apart as if he were getting ready to frisk me in our dining room. He ran his hands all up and down my sides while his hot breath warmed my neck. "You so thick, baby girl. I swear I ain't never seen no woman with a body like this, and it drives me insane because you only eighteen. Fresh."

He licked my neck, reached around, and unbuttoned my pants, sliding them down my legs. As soon as they were at my ankles, he didn't even allow me to kick them off. He simply forced his face into my cheeks before taking his tongue and licking down my crease, grunting loudly while massaging my ass. "Mm, baby, you smell so good. Don't nobody smell like my baby. I love this body so much."

I arched my back and felt him open my cheeks and begin to suck on my kitty through my thong underwear. I closed my eyes tight as they rolled into the back of my head. "Idris, please. I'm tired. I just wanna get some sleep. We can do this at another time. Please," I begged as he pulled my crotch band to the side and licked in between my sex lips, pulling on them with his lips and sucking on my jewel in such a way I couldn't help moaning out loud. I hated myself because I knew that would encourage him, and I honestly wanted him to stop. But it was like I said before, this man had a spell over my body. One I couldn't understand or break. It was like I hated when he touched me, but while he did it I felt like I was in another dimension. A dimension where the pleasure was immense as long as I didn't focus in on the facts, and that was so hard because I loved my mother so much, and she loved him. I didn't like the way my body responded to his ministrations. I felt like I was betraying her and my sister.

Idris smacked me on my butt with his open hand, causing me to yelp out in pain. "I told you that ain't my name for you. You call me daddy because you my baby girl now." *Whap*! He smacked me again, this time a little harder. "Who am I?" *Whap*!

"Daddy! You my daddy! I'm so sorry, Daddy! Please don't hit me no more," I cried as the tears sailed down my cheeks.

I felt him grab my wrists and place them in handcuffs, clicking them tight before pushing me back against the wall, kicking my legs apart, kneeling down, and putting his face against my ass. "I'm finna make you scream my name, baby girl. We gon' nip this shit in the bud right now. I ain't finna stop until you get it through yo' head just who I am."

Jelissa

He grabbed me by the waist, and the next thing I felt was him sucking both of my sex lips into his mouth while he pinched my clitoris and rubbed it in circles vigorously.

I couldn't hold back. As much as I hated myself, I had to let my moans go. I felt like my head was going to explode. "Un! Un! Un! Ah, Daddy! Please! No! Un! Un! Uh, shit! Daddy! Um. Ah!"

He sucked and licked, flicked his tongue back and forth across my clit while two of his fingers ran in and out of me rapidly. My knees felt weak, and the handcuffs around my wrists for some reason were adding to my bliss. I didn't know what was going on inside of me. All I knew was that I was about to explode, and it was all his fault.

"Come on, baby girl. Cum for Daddy! Cum for me!" He smacked my ass, then forced his face even deeper into my cheeks and started to go crazy back there. He was suckin' and licking so many of my parts I couldn't hold back any longer, as much as I wanted to. And believe me, I tried.

"Uh! Daddy!" I screamed and came, bouncing my ass back into his face while he smacked it and licked up and down my crack before sucking on my pearl roughly. That sent me into another wave of tremors.

The next thing I knew he picked me up and carried me to my mother's room and tossed me on the bed. He took one of the handcuffs off my right wrist, only to click it onto the headboard. Then he reached into the nightstand, pulled out another pair, and handcuffed my left wrist before straddling me and ripping my Prada blouse down the middle, along with my bra. He tossed them behind him, leaned down, and sucked my left nipple into his mouth while cupping my right breast.

"Mm, I love this body. I'm obsessed with it. You belong to me, Leesee. I'm Daddy. I gotta have you, baby. I need you. Don't you understand that?" While he sucked on my breast, he ran his fingers up and down pussy, playing with the lips before sliding two fingers deep into my center.

42

Love Me Even When It Hurts

"Uh. Daddy. Please let me go. I'm tired. What if my mama come home early?" I moaned.

In response, his fingers went deeper into me, and his thumb ran circles around my protruding clitoris. "I need you to want me, baby. I need you to want Daddy in the same way I want you. You're my Leesee. Mine. You belong to me and only me. I'll kill any muthafucka who tells me otherwise." He squeezed both of my breasts, then slid down my body and sucked my lips into his mouth once again while he massaged my breasts roughly.

It was driving me insane, as much as I hated to admit it. He trapped my clit with his teeth and nipped at it lightly before sucking it into his thick lips. I humped off the bed into his face. "Uh! Daddy! You're making me! You're making me! Uh! I'm beggin' you. Ah!" I screamed at the top of my lungs. Then the tears started to fall down my cheeks because I felt so guilty, but I couldn't control my body. I fought against the handcuffs but to no avail, while Idris sucked at me like a straight savage of a man. "I'm cumming, Daddy. I'm cumming!"

He sucked harder on my clit and fingered me deeper. My juices coated his face and the palm of his hand. Then he straddled me and began to rub his big penis head up and down my slit. "Tell me that you need me, Leesee. Tell Daddy you want him to put his dick in you and go hard. Tell me, baby. I need to hear it."

He took his pipe and rubbed it all over my lips and clit. I was so riled up I was humping upward into his tool. I needed *it* inside of me. Every thing in me was screaming for it.

"Tell me, baby girl! Now!"

I hated myself for the next words that I uttered. "Please put it in me, Daddy. Please. Fuck yo' baby girl. I'm begging you. I need it so – uh!"

I screamed as I felt him slam into me with so much force. He was rocking my lower region as hard as he could. His pole slid through my lips and tunneled its way into my stomach, only to be pulled out and shoved into me again and again. *Bam. Bam. Bam.*

Jelissa

"This. My. Pussy. Leesee. You. Hear. Me? I'm yo' daddy, baby. Yours. We belong. To. Each. Other." *Bam. Bam. Bam.*

He tossed my thighs onto his forearms and started working me over like never before while tears rolled down my cheeks and dripped from my chin. I closed my eyes and couldn't help screaming because it hurt but felt so good at the same time. The bed rocked back and forth, causing the headboard to slam into the wall violently.

"Daddy. Daddy. Please. Please. Slow down. Uh! You killing me! Uh. It feels so good! I can't take it. I can't take it! Um! I'm cumming! I'm cumming!" I screamed. "Uh!"

He sped up the pace and really put his back into it. His chest muscles rippled as he crashed into me. I opened my eyes in time to see his ab muscles lock up, then I felt his cream hitting my walls. For some reason that sent me into another orgasm right before the guilt set again.

"I love you, baby girl. I love you. Tell Daddy you love him, too. Tell me right now!" he hollered, pumping more of his cream into me.

"I love you, Daddy. I love you so much. I do," I whispered, out of breath with sweat dripping down my forehead.

He leaned down and kissed my lips, and we started to make out loudly, though he was doing most of the work. I knew whenever he was just about done he loved to rain kisses on me, so I went with the flow, though I felt so dirty and guilty for betraying my family. My pussy continued to percolate as I felt his member getting harder inside me as we kissed like high school sweethearts.

Thirty minutes later he lay on his back with me on top of him while he caressed my ass, opening the cheeks and running his fingers in between them. I could smell the scent of our sex in the air, and I was wondering how he was going to get rid of it before my mother got home.

He squeezed my booty and bit into my neck. "You so damn thick, li'l girl, you know that?" he asked, gripping my ass with two hands, one cheek in each.

Love Me Even When It Hurts

I shrugged my shoulders. "Yeah, I guess. I mean, you do tell me that all the time. Is that a bad thing?" I asked naively.

He trailed his finger down to my pussy's opening from the back and slid his digit inside me. "Nall, that's a real good thing. You ten times finer than your mother was when she was your age. That's something to be proud of, because she used to have all the dudes at our school going through it. I mean she even had me like that, but back then she ain't really give me no play. She was all wrapped up in your father, Rah'nell." He shook his head. "It's all good now, though, because I got a better version of her right here, and your li'l box killing what's between her legs. I know you don't probably wanna hear that, but what's real is real." He kissed me on the forehead and continued to push and pull his finger in and out of me. I could hear my kitty making wet, squelchy sounds.

I took a deep breath. "Daddy, can I ask you something without you getting mad or wanting to punish me?" I was worried because I knew Idris had a bad temper and the littlest of things could set him off, especially after he came. See, before he got between my legs, he was always the most kind and gentle person I had ever known. But after he came he seemed to become more angry for some reason, so I knew I had to tread lightly or risk him whooping my ass fo' real.

"Go ahead, baby girl. You can ask me anything, and I'll keep it real wit' you." He kissed my neck, then sucked on my earlobe, before sliding his tongue inside of it, sending chills down my spine. He patted my booty, then squeezed it. "Go ahead."

I bit into my bottom lip and sighed. "Okay, but remember I'm just asking because I want to know what's really good."

He kissed my cheek. "A'ight."

"Daddy, why do you desire my body so much? Like, why don't you pour all the love and affection into my mother the way you do me? Wouldn't that make you guys' relationship more strong?" I asked, started to shake because I was worried he was getting ready to blow up.

He laughed. "It's simple, really. To me you are a new and improved version of her. You're way finer. You're more shapely. Smarter. And if I was at your school, I would have made it my bidness to make sure you were my woman. When your mother was your age, she was caught up on Rah'nell. She shitted on me a lot, and it was because of her that me and that fool never got along. I see you, and I see what she used to be, and it takes me back to my childhood. You make me feel young again. Like I got a fresh start. That's why I'm not playin' about you, and I'll kill any nigga I find sniffing around you, word is bond. The only man you gon' ever be wit' is me. I mean that shit. Do you understand that?" He grabbed a handful of my hair and wrapped it into his fist, pulling my head down to him so I could answer him with my forehead against his.

"Yes, Daddy, I hear you. I hear you loud and clear. I swear I do," I whimpered, feeling my neck get an instant kink inside of it. It hurt so bad at that angle that I needed him to just calm down.

"Now, like I said, you my baby girl now. And I own this body. If I ever catch you fucking wit' somebody other than me, I'ma kill them first, and then yo' ass. Because what we got is sealed in blood. Get me?" He pulled on my hair even harder.

"Yes, Daddy! Yes, I get you! I'm sorry. Just tell me what to do," I cried, feeling trapped and scared for my life. All the things he was saying to me were freaking me out. How was I supposed to be with him for the rest of my life when he was my mother's fiancé and my sister's father? Why wasn't I allowed to date guys my own age? Did he expect me to really be the high school version of my mother forever? What about my future?

"Reach behind you and put my dick back into this wet pussy and ride me nice and slow while you tell me how much you really love yo' daddy. Come on, baby."

Love Me Even When It Hurts

He grabbed my booty and lifted me up a little bit while I reached behind my backside, took ahold of his pipe, and slowly guided the head back into me before riding him in slow motion.

"Tell me, baby."

"I love you, Daddy. Mm. I love you so, so much. Yes," I whimpered with both of my hands against his muscular chest. Every time I rose and fell on his pipe, I felt more and more like dirt. I tried to not focus on the pictures of my mother and him that were all around the room. I tried to not focus on the fact her silk Victoria's Secret nightgown lay right on the loveseat just a little ways from where our heads were.

Rubbed my booty and sucked my nipples, alternating between the two of them. "Yes, baby! Yes! Ride Daddy! Ride yo' daddy, baby. Mm. Shit, yeah!" he groaned, forcing me to ride him faster and faster.

"Oh my god! What the fuck is going on in here?" Nia yelled, bustin' through the bedroom door with Jamal on the side of her.

I fell off Idris and wrapped the sheet around my body. "Nia, I can explain. I swear, I was just –"

Before I could finish my sentence, she jumped onto the bed on top of me and started to swing at me with closed fists. "You fuckin' my daddy, bitch! You dirty bitch. I knew you was fuckin' my daddy! I hate you! I hate yo' ho ass !"

She continued to swing while I blocked her attacks. Every now and then a punch would land on my face, but it didn't do enough damage to hurt me in even the least bit. I was so shocked at being caught that my adrenalin was pumping full blast.

She yanked the sheet off me, exposing my nude body, and that's when I kicked up at her, catching her in the stomach and causing her to topple over after letting out a whoosh of air. "Damn, let me explain. Why don't you just give me a chance?" I pleaded with tears running down my cheeks.

Jelissa

Idris got out of the bed and picked her up, taking her from the room and into her own. I could hear them arguing with one another, but the words weren't so clear that I could make them all out.

Meanwhile, Jamal had his eyes locked in on me as if I was his last meal. He dragged his eyes up and down my body, then kept them pinned on my pussy, licking his lips. "I knew you was bad under them clothes, but I never knew you was this fine. Damn, you fine!" he said, shaking his head in amazement.

I grabbed the sheet off the bed and wrapped it around me. "Can you get out of here, please? My sister is in the other room. Get out!" I yelled.

His eyes bugged out of his head. "Aw, yeah. That's my bad." He made his way out of the door, but not without sniffing the air as if he were a dog or some shit.

As soon as he stepped out of the door, Nia shot past him and came back into the room, her eyes filled to the brim with tears. "How long, Leesee? How long you been fuckin' my father? Please, that's all I wanna know." She wiped the tears from her cheeks.

Idris stormed into the room and picked her up, carrying her back into the room they had come out of while her legs kicked at the air wildly. I simply lowered my head and felt sick to my stomach. I knew the shit was about to hit the fan as soon as my mother got home, and I wasn't prepared for what would come next.

Chapter 5

Rome

Kazi stepped on the gas and looked at me with a mug on his face. "Now that we dropped that bitch-ass nigga off to Capo and his boys, we gotta handle one of the li'l niggaz I just got the go-ahead to knock off. It's like I keep on telling you, you can't even begin to understand what the game is until you get yo' first body. So after I hem this nigga up, I'ma have you pull the trigger and knock this nigga head off. Soon as you taste that first blood, it ain't gon' be no turning back for you. Trust me when I tell you that. We got the same blood coursing through our veins, so I know." He handed me the bag of Whoppers. "Huh, put some food on yo' stomach, and don't be acting like no bitch when we get over here. This nigga stay wit' a few of his family members, so I might have to pave the way before you get yo' first murder, a'ight?" He looked me over real closely with his upper lip curled.

I was feeling sicker than somebody with the flu. I'd just watched my brother and a few of the dudes from Bergen Street drag Paper into a warehouse where he was dropped on the ground in front of a group of about ten other niggaz. As soon as they dropped him on the ground, my brother shook up with some heavyset dude with long dreads before coming back out to his truck and smashin' away from there. He even left the dudes who had helped him get Paper to the warehouse. I didn't fully understand what was going on at that point, but I felt like I was way over my head.

I wished I was back at the crib in my own bed. I ain't wanna kill nobody for no reason at all. That shit just seemed stupid to me, and I didn't know how to tell my brother that without him going over the deep end and spazzing out on me. So, instead of speaking my mind, all I did was swallow my spit and dig a Whopper out of the bag of food.

Jelissa

Fifteen minutes later, we rolled over to Thompson Drive and my brother parked his truck four houses over from the one where our target resided. The sun was just starting to set and the wind had picked up considerably. I could hear it howling outside the whip.

My brother pointed at Audi's house. "That fool stay right there. He still live wit' his people, so it's finna be fucked up for them, but I ain't got nothin' to do wit' that. All this shit is a part of the game. You gon' learn that in due time." He seemed to zone out looking at the house. "Yeah, it's all a part of the game, Rome. You stay right here, and when I'm ready for you, I'ma come on the porch and wave you over. I know you ain't got no experience in this kick-do' part, so fall back and just let me handle my bidness."

He reached under his seat and came up with the same Glock .40 he'd popped Paper with before opening the door to his truck and jumping out, running along somebody's gangway who lived four houses over. I watched him leave a track of Timberland boot prints in the snow before he disappeared into the back of the house.

The snow seemed to fall harder, but that didn't stop my hands from sweating like crazy. I rubbed them over the legs of my pants and tried to calm myself down by rapping a few Yo Gotti lyrics to myself, but even that wasn't doing the trick. The fact of the matter was Kazi expected me to kill somebody that night, and I was sure I didn't have that in me like he did.

I took the .38 special from under the seat and looked the gun over in my hand. It looked beasty and felt heavy. I couldn't believe it was supposed to be the first gun I was supposed to use to take somebody's life. A life I didn't even know. I exhaled loudly and started to shake like crazy. Closing my eyes, I tried to imagine the face of my mother. I missed her so much. I was hoping when I got home I would at least be able to get a hug from her, but I knew that was wishful thinking.

When I opened my eyes, I saw Kazi was on the porch waving me over. I didn't know how long he had been doing it, but just imagining it was more than a few seconds caused me to freak out a little bit before I jumped out of the whip, ducked down, and made my way over to where he was.

As soon as I got onto the porch he snatched me up and pressed his forehead into mine. "Nigga, don't get to freaking out when you get in here. Just go wit' the flow. I had to take care of my bidness. Shit happens." He nudged me a li'l bit so I would walk into the house.

I wasn't more than ten feet inside of it before I stepped into their living room and saw an older man who must've been in his late fifties sat on the white leather couch with blood dripping from a hole in his forehead. In front of him on the big smart-screen television was an NBA game, the New Jersey Nets versus the Miami Heat.

"That old dude be a'ight. He ain't have them many years left on his life, anyway. Come on, le'ts go," he demanded, bumping me out of the way.

I followed him through the house until we got into the kitchen, and right there in the middle of the floor was an older woman around the same age as the old man. She lay up against the stove with a hole in her chest, eyes wide open. Blood ran out of her wound as if it were a faucet.

I swallowed and shook my head as Kazi walked to the back door and flung it open, then took the stairs up to the attic. Once we got all the way up there, I saw the lights were on and there was a dude lying on a bed with duct tape on his mouth and hands. For some reason he was ass-naked, lying face-downward, flopping around like a fish fresh out of water.

Beside him was a female with long, curly hair, dark skin, and a real pretty face, though it had a small scar on the side of her right cheek. I'd seen her with my brother on more than one occasion, though I'd never spoken a word to her.

She stood up and slid her Timbs onto her small feet after zipping up her Fendi bomber jacket. "Yo, kid, make sure you body this nigga fo' me, too. Nigga don't understand that no means no, nah mean?" She walked over to

51

Jelissa

Kazi and hugged him for a few moments. "Where you parked at? Cuz this nigga drove me here, cuz."

He brought her over to the window and I guessed pointed at his truck parked a little way down the street. "We ain't that far away. I ain't trying to be up here all day. I just want my li'l nigga to body this chump so we can cross this off fo' Capo. Kid gotta taste his first blood, and he about to do that shit right now. Help me sit this fuck-nigga up against the headboard."

I watched as they went to work, struggling with Audi until they had his back against the headboard. Then Kazi looked over to me, while he held his gun out for me to grab. "Huh, you can't use that .38. This one got a silencer on it. That way the neighbors don't get involved. Come on over here and handle this bidness."

I slowly made my way over to him, and Audi screamed into his duct tape. I didn't know what he was saying, but I imagined he was begging for his life. It's what I would have been doing in that moment. I grabbed the gun from Kazi and looked him in his eyes, feeling like I was getting ready to shit on myself.

Kazi held Audi more firmly against the headboard. "Look, Rome, this bitch-nigga is a snitch. He one of the lowest kind of human beings that trap through the slums. Now, if I don't body this chump, then every nigga he told on gon' come fo' our heads. That's mine, yours, and mama's. We can't have that shit. That ain't how our bloodline work, so I want you to put two holes right here." He pointed to Audi's forehead, touching it in two different spots right by each other.

"Yeah, son. Knock moneybrains out so we can be up out this bitch. Word is bond, I gotta get over to the projects and collect my scratch before muthafuckas get to spending up my shit. Nah mean? It'll be more bloodshed before the night is over if I don't get there in time, so handle yo' bidness, li'l homie."

I felt my heart beating so fast I was about to pass out. Shit was spinning all around me, and my knees began to buckle. I tried to steady myself as best I could.

52

Love Me Even When It Hurts

Kazi lowered his eyes into slits, mugging me with hatred.

"Yo, Kazi, li'l dawg looking like he about to shit himself. Word is bond, I think this too much for 'im. Just let me body this nigga and we can get a move on. I mean, you already had me fuck 'im and all," the female said, shaking her head.

I was shaking so bad that I felt stupid. I didn't wanna kill this nigga for no reason. I didn't want to be haunted by his spirit for the rest of my life. That shit seemed pointless. It wasn't in me.

Kazi lowered his eyes into slits and bit into his bottom lip before pulling out another Glock, cocking it, then slamming the barrel to the female's head and pulling the trigger twice. *Boom! Boom!* Her head jerked backward twice before she fell to the floor in a pool of blood.

"You see that? That's how easy it is to kill a muthafucka. It's boom, boom, and you get that shit over wit'. Now get yo' punk ass over here and smoke this nigga before I smoke you like I just did this punk-ass bitch!"

I felt my knees shaking ten times worse than before as I tried my best to step forward. I looked down onto the female as she lay on the floor. I felt scared out of my mind. That was the first time I had ever seen anybody killed in front of me, and it terrified me, especially since it was a female because when it came to murder, I never really imagined them being the ones murdered in the streets like that.

"Come on, Rome. Hurry up and kill this nigga before them people show up!" Kazi growled and held onto Audi more aggressively.

I took two giant steps and wound up standing on the side of the bed next to Kazi. I extended my hand and pressed the barrel to Audi's forehead, all the while saying a silent prayer in my head. *Father, forgive me for this sin. Please don't let me wind up in hell over this. I'm begging you.* I squeezed my eyelids tight and then opened them as I tried to calm myself down. I put my finger on the trigger and imagined this dude had put his hands on my mother.

I imagined he slapped her and tried to force himself on her. As soon as I saw the image in my head, I pulled the trigger. *Boom.*

His head jerked backward and Kazi moved away from his slumped body. I could hear him screaming into the duct tape, and it blew my wig back because I expected him to be dead.

"Hit his bitch-ass again, Rome. Body that nigga. Do it!" Kazi said through clenched teeth.

I felt sick on my stomach, but my adrenalin was pumping like crazy. I pressed the gun to the side of his ear and pulled the trigger again. *Boom.* This time his head jerked violently to the side and his blood squirted like mist into the air, splashing me across the face. He fell out of the bed and to the floor right on top of the female.

"Hell yeah! Now that's what I'm talking about. Let's get the fuck up out of here," Kazi hollered, pulling my arm.

As we rolled home, I sat there in the passenger's seat of my brother's truck, trying my best to not throw up on the dashboard. My stomach felt like I had the flu, and my vision was so blurry I kept on squeezing my eyelids together. I kept imagining the way Audi's head blew open as the bullet went inside of it. The way his head jerked violently to the side before the bloody mist sprayed into the air.

"Yo, word is bond, I'm proud of you, kid. I ain't think you was gon' do it. You gon' be sick for a few days, but after all the night sweats and terrors, you'll be good. You just gotta let that shit pass. What you experiencing right now is called remorse. Every nigga get that the first time they kill somethin'. Trust me, it will pass." He nodded his head. "Still can't believe you finally got yo' first one. Hell yeah!" He turned up the radio, blasting some Jay-Z and nodding his head as if he were already in a whole different world.

When we got home that night, my mother met us at the door in her Burberry robe. As soon as she opened it, she hugged my brother and he picked her up, walking her into the living room as she kissed his face before he put her down. I kicked the door closed and stepped inside, taking shallow breaths to calm myself down.

She kissed him on the lips and lay her head on his chest. "So, tell me what's good. Did he have enough guts to handle his bidness, or did he chicken out?" she asked, looking me up and down with a look of disgust on her face. I could tell she was counting me out before he even gave her a response.

Kazi put his arm around her neck and kissed her on the forehead. "Nall, he ain't chicken out. I mean it took some nudging, but he knocked that nigga head off. Two bullets straight to the dome, no mercy-style. Ain't you proud of him?" he asked, lookin' down at her, then kissing her on the forehead.

She curled her lip and looked me over with distaste. "Not really. I know you probably did most of the work. Probably held his finger on the trigger and pulled it yo'self. Either way, it's about time he grew the fuck up. But nall, I ain't impressed, and this is most definitely awkward," she said, turning around to look up at him with her gray eyes that she had also given me.

My brother's were dark brown like our father's. I never understood why I didn't get those manly eyes that they had. All through grade school the boys used to make fun of my eyes and said they made me look like a pretty boy. I used to hate that. It was the reason I got into so many fights when I was little.

"What's the matter, Mama? What's awkward?" Kazi asked.

She bit into her bottom lip. "Because I thought he was going to fail at this whole thing and we wouldn't allow him in the house tonight. But now that he handled his bidness, that's throwing off what I had in mind, because I need to holler at you on some personal notes." She said the last part so low I was almost unable to hear her clearly.

My brother lowered his eyes. "Some' personal? What you talking about? Why wouldn't you be able to holler at me while he's…? Oh, okay. Okay. I see what you saying."

Jelissa

He started laughing. "Yo, Rome, you gon' have to make other arrangements tonight. Maybe you can chill in my truck until I come out and get you. You know, turn the heat on and shit. But moms need me, and I'm the man of the house. You gotta respect that."

I heard everything they were saying, but I was still so fucked up I couldn't think straight. I needed some fresh air, and I didn't even care what they were about to do. I took the keys from my brother as the room continued to spin around me. He walked me back to the front door with his arm around my mother.

"Don't drive off in my shit. Just chill in there and get you a few hours of sleep or something. I'll be out there to wake you up in like, what, two hours, Ma?" He looked down at her with a curious look on his face.

She shrugged her shoulders. "I don't know, baby. Let's just play it by ear. He'll be alright, though."

My brother had parked his truck in the back of the house, right where our garage would have been had it not been burned down back in the summer of 2018. I took the gangway into the backyard, and before I could get half-way there I gagged and threw up all along the side of the house. I imagined how the female's brains looked shooting out of her head, then Audi's body when it fell right on top of her dead one. Even though it was freezing cold outside, I was sweating profusely.

I wished I had anybody at that time who I could have went to, anybody within the vicinity who actually loved me and would have allowed me to break down in front of them. I felt so alone and so lost.

I stood up, wiped my mouth with the back of my hand, and continued on my path to the back of my house. Once there I could hear the commotion from the neighbors next door. It sounded like they were arguing intensely.

Chapter 6

Leesee

My mother grabbed me by the neck and slammed me into the dining room wall. She slapped me so hard I yelped out in pain. "You backstabbing li'l bitch! How dare you fuck my fiancé? How dare you fuck him in my bed?" She smacked me again, then pushed me to the floor.

I held my face while I looked up at her. I was terrified she was going to kill me. My mother, for the most part, was a very calm woman, but then there were times when she'd lose her cool, and that's when she'd transform into a whole different person. On more than one occasion she'd beaten the crap out of both me and my sister Nia because of us fighting one another. When she got down she had a tendency of messing us up physically. So yeah, I was afraid of her, especially considering the circumstances.

"Mama, I'm sorry. I swear I didn't mean it. Please forgive me," I begged.

I watched her take her Ferragamo belt out of its loopholes and wrap it around her hand before whipping it through the air and connecting with the side of my face. *Whap*! I screamed as the pain stung me. I got ready to get up, and that's when she grabbed a handful of my hair and committed to beating me with everything she had while she told me how much of a whore I was and that she hated me for betraying her like that. *Whap*! *Whap*! *Whap*! She beat me until her arm gave out.

I had welts all over my body and face. She stood over me, breathing hard. "Bitch, for the rest of the time you're in my house, you betta not say one fucking word to me or I'm going to kill you. Do you hear me?" she asked with tears running down her cheeks.

I scooted backward on my butt as snot ran out of my nose and into my mouth. "Yes, ma'am."

Jelissa

She frowned. "And when my man get home from work, you betta not say a word to him because I know you been seducing him. I know he would never fall for you, little girl, unless you was takin' advantage of me because I have to work so much. I can't believe you would do me like this. You broke my heart."

She fell to a sitting position, breaking down and crying tears of pain before pointing down the hall. "Go to yo' room. And I meant what I said."

That night I didn't get one wink of sleep. When Idris got home I listened to him and my mother argue for three hours straight. Apparently my sister had given her the full rundown of what she'd caught us doing, and to my amazement Idris didn't deny the fact. His excuse was he was lonely because she was never home and I was way too affectionate with him. That he'd lost himself because I looked so much like her.

Now, I knew that was bullshit, and it hurt me to hear. I felt so trapped, dazed, and confused. I didn't know what to do or what to think. I wanted to run away from home, but I didn't have anywhere to go. And even if I did, I didn't have the money to get there.

The longer they argued, the sicker I became until I couldn't take it anymore. I got out of the bed and slipped into my Fendi pants and sweater, then my Ugg boots. I opened my window and got ready to climb out of it. It wasn't that much of a drop due to the fact my room was on the first floor. I simply needed some fresh air, so I figured I'd walk around in the backyard for a while until I could clear my head. I got my entire body out of the window and dangled for a brief moment before I let go. A second later I landed in a big pile of snow right on my butt, got up, and dusted myself off.

As soon as I stood up, all the water works started. I cried so hard I could barely breathe. I hated myself for being so weak. I hated my life. I hated the way Idris constantly went in on me, breaking down my defenses until I was at his mercy. I hated myself for feeling the things I felt whenever he did those things to my body. I hated myself for being able to feel the pleasure I felt. I felt sick, and now my mother hated my guts along with my sister. I didn't have anything to live for other than my father, and I needed him so freaking bad.

I fell to my knees and kept on crying. The harsh wind blew into my face, trying its best to freeze my tears. It took some of my breath away, but I kept on crying, feeling lower than dirt. Lower than scum. Why did Idris want me so bad? Why couldn't he just allow me to be a young woman? Why couldn't he simply love my mother and leave me alone? Why was I forced to go through all of those challenges? I was just a kid. Life wasn't fair, and I never had a chance. I loved my mother and sister so much and I needed them both, yet in one night I'd not lost one, but the both of them, and I truly felt they would never love me again. That thought was almost too much for me to handle.

I took one look back at the house and decided right then I was out of there. I couldn't take it anymore. I could still hear my mother and Idris inside, arguing at the top of their lungs. I shook my head and walked to the back of our yard, opened the gate right alongside our garage, then ran out of it and into the alley at full speed. I didn't know where I was going to go. All I knew was I could no longer stand to be there.

As I got into the alley, the snow blew into my face, nearly blinding me. I squinted my eyes and started to run again, looking over my shoulder at the distance I'd gone away from home, feeling my stomach doing somersaults. I must've not been looking where I was going because as I was turning my head to look forward, I found myself crashing into the back of the neighbor's truck hard and with so much velocity I fell to my butt. "Ow!" I yelled, holding my chest. It felt like I'd been kicked in it.

The driver's door opened and out jumped Rome. His eyes were wide open, and I noted they were wet with what I assumed were tears. He rushed over to my side and knelt down, extending me a hand. "Leesee, is that you?" he asked with a look of concern. The snow blew into his face,

Jelissa

sticking to it. At the same time it caused him to flutter his eyelids. I could tell he was cold, especially since all he had on was a black polo t-shirt.

I allowed him to help me to my feet. "Yeah, it's me. What are you doing out here at this time of night?" I asked, dusting my butt off, then rubbing along the front of my chest. I could tell there would be some bruising there. It screamed agony.

He wiped his face with his left hand. "I'm going through somethin' right now. I just needed some fresh air. I feel like I'm losing my mind." He lowered his head and shook it. "What about you?"

I took a deep breath and could not stop the tears from falling down my cheeks. I could feel the welts my mother had left all over my body, and that mixed with the pain in my chest as well as the pain in my heart. I damn near fainted. "I'm so hurt right now. I thought about running away from home, but I don't know where to go. My whole family hates me," I whimpered.

Rome stepped forward and wrapped his big arms around me before I could stop him. Prior to this night all we'd ever done was say hi to each other in passing. On more than one occasion I'd witnessed how his family did him, but I was unsure if he knew even the slightest about my own family life. For some reason his arms made me feel so safe and secure. Maybe it was the fact he didn't know how bad I'd screwed over my mother and sister, how much of a disgrace I was.

"There, there, Leesee. It's going to be okay. I don't really know what's wrong, but I swear I will do anything I can to make you feel all better. I don't like seeing you break down like this. It can't be as bad as all that," he uttered, holding me tight with his muscular arms.

I could smell his cologne, and once again it made me feel safe. I wrapped my arms around his waist and lay my head on his chest. "You don't understand. I betrayed my mother and my sister. They hate me now. I don't have any family left, and my mother said she doesn't even want to speak to me again. My life is over," I cried, now starting

60

to get cold. The snow really started to come down. The wind howled loudly and nearly pushed us over. I could feel Rome shaking like crazy while he held me, and I knew he had to be cold, but he didn't let me go. He hung on.

"Well, once again, I don't know what you did, and I don't even care. Your life is not over, and you don't have to run away. I'll do anything to make you feel better. I'll hold you all night if I have to. I swear I will," he said, shaking like crazy.

I tightened my arms around him and tried to look up into his face, but the snow was falling way too hard, the wind blowing as if it had something against the both of us. "Rome, why are you huggin' me like this when you barely even know me? Why do you even care? I'm just a nobody. Nobody loves me anymore. I'm trash," I said with tears falling. Now I was beginning to shake like a leaf. I could feel him holding me tighter.

"You're not trash, Leesee. You're beautiful, and I care even if nobody else does. I don't care what you've done or how many people hate you. I never will. You're special to me. You always have been," he said, leaning down and kissing me on the forehead.

I felt like my soul melted as I felt his hot lips land on my cold forehead. His affection warmed my heart, and for that brief kiss it caused me to feel halfway decent. I didn't really know him as a person, but I was thankful for his kind words and the way he was holding me.

"Leesee! Leesee! Girl, where are you?!" came Idris' voice.

I could tell he was at our backdoor somewhere. Just hearing his voice caused me to jump out of my skin. My heart started to beat super fast. I tried to unleash myself from Rome's big arms, but it was too late. Before I could get out of them, Idris stepped into the alley with a scowl on his face that said he was thinking murder. He mugged us and started to walk over to where we were, and still Rome did not let me go until he walked over and yanked me away by my arm.

Jelissa

"Let her the fuck go, li'l nigga, before I body you out here tonight," he growled, pulling me behind him.

"Daddy, it's okay. I was just going for a walk, and he saw me and was trying to make me feel –"

Whack! He backhanded me so fast it caught me off guard. I flew into the truck before landing on my back with blood coming out of my mouth. Rome rushed him right away, but before he could get all the way to him Idris pulled out a .9 millimeter service weapon, stopping him in his tracks. Rome threw his hands in the air and gave Idris the look of death. "Yo, you shouldn't be putting yo' hands on her like that, Shotgun. That's a li'l female. She was already out here breaking down and stuff, man. This ain't cool."

Idris walked closer to Rome and put the gun directly in his face. "You bitch-ass nigga, you don't worry about what I do to my daughter or what she going through because she belongs to me, and I'll kill any muthafucka who tells me she don't. I betta not never catch you touching her again, or I swear to God on everything I love, I'm gon' body every muthafucka that's kin to you after I knock yo' brains out yo' skull. Don't think just 'cause I'm the police I ain't still bout' that life. Word is bond, I murk niggaz like you every single day." He curled his upper lip and turned his pistol sideways in Rome's face.

Rome swallowed and frowned. "Like I said, that's a li'l female, and you shouldn't be putting yo' hands on her like that." He looked down to me. "You okay, Leesee?"

Idris snapped. "Ah! You bitch-ass nigga! What part of this shit don't you get?" He pressed the gun to Rome's cheek and curled his nose. "I'll stank you right here, boy. Now, I'm gon' tell you one mo' time: don't worry about her because she belongs to me. You got that?" he asked through clenched teeth and with his cheek against Rome's.

I looked to my right and saw Kazi coming out of the back of their house in his boxers and a white beater. "Aye! What the fuck going on out here, Shotgun? Get the fuck off my brother!" he yelled, running in the snow with two pistols in his hands. Behind him their mother stood in the doorway with a robe wrapped around her.

Idris reached down and snatched me up by my arm just as Kazi got over to us. "Let's go, li'l girl." He pushed me in front of him and looked over his shoulder at Rome. "If I ever catch you fucking wit' her again, I'ma kill you, nigga. Now try me."

Rome held his silence, but never took his eyes away from my own. That night I saw somethin' in them I had never seen from any male before in regards to me. I saw he wasn't about to bow down. There was a need for me in his eyes, and it caused the hairs on my body to stand up. As Idris snatched me away from him, I felt deep within my soul that I needed him just as much.

Instead of Idris taking me upstairs back into the house with my mother and sister, he took me downstairs and into the basement. Once there he closed the door behind us, picked me up, and threw me on the bed that folded out from the couch. "Bitch, you betta not say nothing. I'm ti'ed of you playin' wit' me. You really don't understand what I mean when I say you belong to me and only me, do you?" He straddled me and started to force me out of my coat and clothes, ripping my Fendi top and bra off of me, then taking me out of my pants and panties.

"Idris, please stop. Please, don't do this. My mother already mad at me. My sister hates me. I am begging you. Have mercy."

"Shut yo' ass up. I ain't trying to hear none of that shit." He reached behind him and pulled out his handcuffs before cuffing my wrists one at a time to the pipe that went along the brick wall slightly above the couch bed. Once that was done, he forced my legs apart and got in between them, taking his clothes off in a frenzy. "You keep calling me Idris when I already told yo' ass what my name was when it comes to you. I'm Daddy. You belong to me. But you can't get that shit through yo' head, so I'm gon' fuck it into you."

After he was naked, he got up and disappeared for a few seconds, then came back and put a strip of duct tape over my mouth. "I'm finna fuck you until it's time for you to get up and go to school, then when you get home I'm gon' fuck you some more. And I'm gon' keep on fucking you until you get it through yo' head that I'm the only man you gon' ever need and you gon' ever be able to have. I swear to God, I'll kill you, Leesee. I'll kill you because you belong to me, and I ain't sharing you. You were created to be my baby girl. All mines."

He ducked between my legs and forced them wide apart before eating my kitty like a maniac, sucking on the lips roughly and nipping at my clit harder than ever. I prayed my mother didn't come downstairs and find us this way. I knew she would blame me. I knew she would attack me and probably kill me this time.

Idris didn't waste much time getting me ready. He sat up, took his piece, and forced it inside me, implanting himself deep within my womb before he started to really do me hard and fast while I screamed into my duct tape and fought against the handcuffs to no avail.

"You're mine, Leesee. You belong to me! Uh, shit. I'll kill a nigga over you. You're never gonna leave me. I'll kill you first! You hear me?" he growled, fucking me so fast and hard I couldn't think straight. I did everything I could to twist and turn and try to get him up off me, but it seemed my attempts only excited him more and more.

True to his word, he didn't get off me until the sun was coming up. To this day I still don't understand why my mother never came down to the basement looking for us. I mean, Idris' car was parked in front of the house, which meant he couldn't have been that far away.

Before he finally released me, he grabbed my face and held it in his hand, squeezing it tightly. "If I ever catch you fucking with another nigga again, it'll be yo' last time. I'ma kill your mama first, then Nia, and then I'm coming for you. I swear to God, this ain't a game. You are my property. Now get yo' ass up and get in the shower so you can get to school on time." He leaned in and sucked my lips, then bit into the top one, causing it to bleed. I winced in pain, crying, but he didn't seem to care.

Love Me Even When It Hurts

When I got to the top of the stairs, my mother was at the stove cooking breakfast with my sister at the table looking at her phone. She looked over to me as I stepped past the table and shook her head. "You ain't my daughter no more, Leesee. I don't give a fuck what happen to you no more. The only reason I ain't kicking you out right now is because he won't let me. So, from now on he gon' take care of you." She turned her back on me and kept on cooking.

Nia looked up at me and smiled. "I still love you, big sis. I just don't trust you. You trifling as hell. But you need to come on, 'cause we gon' be late for school." She started texting on her phone and got up from the table.

In the bathroom I broke down to my knees in pain. Everything on me felt like it hurt, including my heart. I got up and turned on the shower as hot as I could take it, stripped, and stepped into the tub feeling lower than low.

Jelissa

Chapter 7

Rome

I couldn't get Leesee out of my mind no matter how hard I tried, and trust me, I was trying as best I could. It was the next day after our crazy night, and I found myself sitting in class in a daze. I'd already finished up my exams for the term, so my presence was pointless. At least that's how I felt, but Kazi was making me go because he said every time I missed more than two days of school a week, them people wound up sweating our moms. And after all the shit we had going on with our family, the last thing we needed was the county of Newark all in our bidness. So there I was, sitting in a daze and remembering her beautiful face and those li'l Asian eyes that had drove me crazy since the first day we'd moved next door to them.

The bell rang, so I grabbed my books off the desk and made my way into the crowded halls of the school. There were only a few hours left for the school day, and Kazi was picking me up to drop me off at one of his traps he was gon' have me move heroin out of. I was honestly ready to get money. I was tired of being broke, and since I was only a few months away from turning eighteen, I knew I had to get it together. Didn't no female in Jersey wanna mess wit' a broke nigga, so I had to get my weight up. I had to get my own, that way my mother and brother couldn't keep on locking me out the crib every time they needed to 'holler at each other.' I shook my head at that one.

Since the next hour I had was study hall, I decided to step out of the school and smoke me a blunt just like most kids did. I headed toward the back of Malcolm Shabazz High, opened the door, and was met with the cool wind of winter. Thankfully this day it wasn't snowing so bad. There were only light flurries dropping from the sky, and I could handle that.

Jelissa

I folded up a piece of paper and stuck it into the back of the door so it'd stay propped open while I smoked my blunt. If that door closed, it would have been damn near impossible to get back into the school. They were real strict about entering and exiting the building, so I made sure it didn't close back. The last thing I needed to hear was Kazi's mouth. I just wanted him to take me to the hood and plug me in so I could get right.

After I propped the door, I stepped all the way out of the building and made my way toward the student parking lot, funneling my hand so I could get the blunt to light when I heard a loud-ass scream. I perked up and looked around. Seconds later it happened again, and I heard a female say, "Get off of me!"

I started to jog as little bit, now really searching, looking all around the cars and in between the lanes, and that's when I saw Jamal's punk ass all over Leesee. He had her pressed up against his Navigator, sucking her neck all wild and shit. I dropped my blunt and the lighter and bolted over to them. As soon as I got there, I grabbed this fool and tore him away from Leesee. "Fuck you doing to her?" I hollered, standing in between them, looking back at her and watching her straighten out her clothes.

Jamal walked up into my face and curled his lip. "Nigga, this ain't got nothin' to do wit' you. This li'l bitch right here going. She ain't nothin' but a ho. She fucked her mother's fiancé and everything. I'm just trying to see what's really good." He laughed and made an attempt to reach around me so he could grab her.

I pushed him so hard he flew into the Cadillac Escalade's door that was parked beside his truck. "Bitch-ass nigga, that don't give you no reason to try and rape her."

I turned around to try to make sure she was okay because I could hear her crying behind me, and that's when Jamal rushed me at full speed and tackled me into his truck, squishing Leesee in the process. She screamed out in pain and fell to the ground. Now I was heated. I wrestled with him for a few seconds before gettin' the upper hand. I pushed him as hard as I could away from me, then punched him square in the nose and hit him with a right hook that connected with his jaw. The sound of fists hitting meat was loud in the parking lot.

He fell to the ground directly on his face, struggling to get up. That's when I saw there was somebody else in his truck. The back door opened and a real heavyset dude got out and threw his guards in the air.

"You want drama, nigga? A'ight, what's good?" he asked, bouncing on his toes. Then he stepped forward and swung, as the other kids in the parking lot started to close in around us.

I jumped back and smacked his fist away, then hit him with a quick jab that caught him in the left eyes. He lowered his head and tried to rush me, but I moved, causing him to run head-first into the body of Jamal's truck. As soon as he did, his neck jerked and he fell backward right into my arms. I picked his ass up as far as I could and fell backward with him, slamming the back of his head into the pavement. *Doom!*

He hollered out in pain and struggled to turn over. Jamal was on his feet, staggering to keep his balance. He held up his guards, then slowly made his way toward me. I could feel my chest getting tight. I was damn near out of breath, but I refused to let these dudes get the better of me. Not in front of Leesee, and not after what I assumed they were getting ready to do to her if I had never shown up.

Leesee stood up and slumped over, holding her stomach. She was in tears, and her blouse was ripped. I made that out through her opened leather Fendi jacket. "Let's just go, Rome. Forget them. I don't want you to get into trouble over me. Please." She reached and pulled my arm.

"Yeah, nigga, you betta listen to that thot-ass bitch. You don't know who you –"

Before he could finish, I was on his ass again. Two to the face, one to the ribs, another to the jaw, then I picked his light-ass up and dumped him on his back before stomping him in the ground with my Timbs. I hated men who took advantage of women. I hated bullies. I hated to see Leesee in tears. I just had to protect her, so I stomped him and stomped him, until his cousin tackled me to the ground and bit me in the back of the neck so hard I hollered out in pain and flung him off me. Turning on my side, I kicked him straight in the stomach and bounced up as the school security guard and Nia ran across the parking lot in our direction.

"Rome, let's go. Come on!" Leesee said, grabbing my arm and pulling me in the opposite direction. Her Jeep was only about nine lanes over. We made it there in no time. She popped the locks and I flung open the passenger's door just as she got in and started the engine, skirting away from the parking space and ultimately out of the school.

As soon as we were on the highway, she turned to me and blinked tears. "Nobody had ever stood up for me like that. I don't understand why you care so much," she said, looking at the road, then back to me.

My heart was beating so fast it was making my chest hurt. I could barely breathe, but all I could care about in that moment was that she was okay. "Are you alright? I saw we crashed into you pretty hard. That's my bad. I should have known better." I lowered my head because looking at her was making me feel a li'l shy. I'd never seen a black woman as fine as she was. Her face was so perfect, even with the little wounds she sustained. Then her skin was the most prettiest shade of brown.

"I'm just fine, thanks to you. Had you not shown up, I'm pretty sure I wouldn't have been. I think they were trying to get me in that truck so they could rape me. At least that's what Jamal kept saying, but instead of saying the word 'rape' he kept saying they were going to 'smash' me." She shook her head. "I'm so tired of being a victim. I wish I wasn't so weak and vulnerable. I wish I knew how to fight back."

That made me feel some type of way. "Long as I'm around, you'll never have to fight for yourself. I'll never let nobody hurt you again if I can help it." I meant every word I told her, too. I wasn't never finna let nobody hurt her again. I'd rather die first. I didn't know why I was feeling like I was, but there was just something about her that brought out that protector in me.

She looked at me for a long time, then smiled weakly, sniffing snot back into her nose. "You don't want to get involved with me, Rome. I'm not right. I'm not the kind of girl you think I am. I'm evil. I'm tainted, and there's nothing really left of me." She started to break down again.

I reached and grabbed her hand, squeezing it. "Come on now, Leesee, you can't believe that. I don't know whose been feeding that garbage into your head but it's not true. I promise you it's not."

She shook her head. "But it is. Every word of it is. I'm no good. You heard what he said about me and my mother's fiancé. It's all true. We were sleeping around together, and now my mother and sister hate me. If he finds out you and I have been together, he's going to kill you. He told me that this morning, and I believe him. He's done it before. He owns me now. My mother gave me to him, and he'll never let me go. Can't you see I'm only placing you in danger?" she whimpered.

A big semi pulled up alongside my window, heavy chunks of snow dropping off the top of it. As the big wheels spun on the road, they slung dirty snow every which way.

Now I was shaking my head. "I don't care about the danger, Leesee. I'm here to protect you for the rest of my life. I'm not scared of Shotgun. There is nothin' he can do to me that I can't do to him. I don't care about your past relationship or whatever you had going on. Nobody can own you unless you allow them to, and I can tell you don't want him to, so I'll fight for you. I'll do whatever it takes to make sure you're never hurt again," I promised, squeezing her hand.

Tears sailed down her cheeks and went into her mouth. She nodded her head and smiled at me. "I believe you. I don't know why, but I do believe everything you're saying." She flipped her hand over and allowed our fingers to interlock, holding the steering wheel with her

71

knees and wiping her tears away with her other hand before pulling into the carpool lane.

This was my first time ever interlocking my fingers with a female, and I thought it would feel a little corny, but for some reason with her it didn't feel that way at all. It actually made me feel as if we were connected in some way.

My phone buzzed. I pulled it out and looked at the face. It was a text message from Kazi asking me where the hell I was. I didn't know how to respond to that, so for the moment I didn't. I turned to Leesee. "So, now that all that is out of the way, what are we going to do? And just know I'm down for whatever as long as you riding beside me."

She took a deep breath and blew it out. "I can't go back home, Rome. I just can't. I don't know where I'm going to go, but I can't go back there. My mother hates me, and so does my sister. Idris won't leave me alone, and he swears up and down I now belong to him. I'm tired of him getting on top of me. I'm tired of submitting myself to him in any way he wants me to. I just can't handle it anymore. I'm close to killing myself, I swear to God!" she screamed before breaking down, her left hand shaking as she drove.

I reached over and stroked her face. "It's okay, Leesee. You don't have to go back there. We'll figure somethin' else out together. Whatever you need me to do, just tell me. I swear to god, I'm not leaving you." I meant that with every fiber of my being.

She nodded. "Well, we're going to need money, no matter what we do. So how much do you have on you?" she asked, turning to look at me.

I felt so stupid because I didn't have a cent to my name, so I lowered my head. "I ain't got nothin' right now. My brother was supposed to link up wit' me after school so he could finally get me started in one of his trap houses. That's where my money was gon' come from. I'm pretty sure he'd still be down for it. I just gotta hit him back and see what's good."

Love Me Even When It Hurts

I picked up my phone and started to text him, letting him know I was ready whenever he was. He hit me right back and told me to meet him at the McDonald's right by my high school. Then I told him it wouldn't be a good idea and I would find a different spot 'cause I had a fight at school. I turned to Leesee. "Can you take me to meet up with my brother? That way I can get some money in my pocket."

She hesitated. "I thought you just said no matter what you weren't going to leave my side?" I could hear her voice cracking up, and that hurt my heart.

"No, no, no. I'm not leaving you like that. I just gotta get some money in my pocket so I can make sure we straight. I can't do nothin' for you if I can't provide a way for us. Am I right?"

She nodded. "Yeah, I guess. But I just don't want to be alone for awhile, so maybe you can get in tune with him tomorrow. Today I just need your support, and tonight I'm gon' need you to hold me as tight as you can. I've never been away from home, especially not overnight, not even at a sleepover. I'm scared out of my mind. So I'm begging you. Please."

I shook my head. "You ain't gotta beg me. I got you. So, where do we go, then? You know, until tomorrow?" I didn't have a clue. Besides my mother and brother, the only other relative I had was an uncle I had not seen in almost five years. The last time I saw him he was smoking crack real bad.

"Well, right now I'm driving over to Halsey Street so I can get a little money from my grandmother. She'll give it to me without asking that many questions. She's the only person outside of my household I trust with my life. My father's mother, and she's always been there for me when I needed her," she smiled.

Ten minutes later we were pulling up in front of a red-bricked home with a burgundy Lincoln Town Car in the driveway and a black Ford F350 parked right behind it. Leesee turned off the ignition and got out of the Jeep. "I'll be right back, okay?" Then I watched her jog up the stairs as the snow started to come down in a blizzard fashion.

My phone buzzed again, and instead of texting back and forth with my brother I picked it up and placed it to my ear. "Bro, I'm taking care of somethin' right now, so I'ma get at you first thing in the morning," I said, feeling the car start to get a lot cooler. I was hoping she wasn't about to be in there for long. The way the snow was coming down, if we didn't get to our final destination for the day, we were going to be trapped and in trouble.

Kazi didn't waste no time at all snapping on me. "Nigga! What the fuck you mean you taking care of somethin'? Yo' bidness is with me today. I'm in charge, and I say you suppose to be in the 'bando getting money. That li'l punk-ass two hunnit you used to ain't gon' cut it. I already told you that. That's disrespectful to my mother and to me for allowing you to bring that shit into the crib. You gotta come better than that, so I'ma show you how. Now, where the fuck you at?"

I felt myself about to lose it. I was so sick of the way he talked to me like I was a wimp or somethin'. I wished I didn't respect him so much, but I did. "Look, bro, some bull crap happened at school. I had to put hands on a couple niggaz, then they called the police, I'm assuming. I caught the niggaz trying to rape Leesee. You know, the female that stay next door to us? And now I'm holding her down until she can feel better. She should be good by the morning time. Is that cool?"

"Cool? Nigga, hell nall, that ain't cool. I'm supposed to let you lay back and be on some Captain Save-A-Ho shit when you can be getting this money for me? Boy, if you don't get yo' ass over here and see what the fuck I'm putting down, we gon' have a serious issues. You sitting yo' ass in that trap today. I already got everything waiting on you. If you want, you can bring her, too. But time is money, so let's get it. Meet me at this address in a half hour." And just like that, the phone call ended.

As soon as he hung up, Leesee came out of her grandmother's house with a scarf wrapped around her face. She opened the driver's door and got in, closing it back behind her. "So look, I kinda told my grandmother a little bit about what happened to me and she says it's cool if I stay here for the night, and you can come in, too, because I told her what you did. I don't know if you'd want to use my Jeep to go and meet up with your brother first, but I wouldn't advise it because the snow looks like it's coming down pretty hard. If you asked me what I wanted you to do, I'd say I just want you to come inside and down to the den with me because I need your arms wrapped around me." She looked into my eyes and bit into her bottom lip all sexy-like, and that's when my phone buzzed again with my brother sweatin' me.

I looked at the face of my phone. It was only three in the afternoon. As much as I wanted to stay there with her, I knew if I didn't meet up with Kazi he'd for sure hunt me down, and when he caught me it'd be hell to pay the captain. But lookin' into her beautiful face was making the latter decision so hard to settle on. I wanted to be all under her the whole night through. I felt like I needed to be, then I started to think about how broke I was. There was no way I could take care of her if I didn't have some form of cash.

I took my hand and rubbed it over my face, then grabbed her hand and kissed it. "Leesee, I swear I don't wanna leave here at all, but I have to. I gotta go out and get some money, that way whenever we decide what we're going to do, I'll be able to hold you down the right way. Kazi wanna show me how to hustle, then put me up in his 'bando. It won't take long before the money is rolling in, and as soon as it does, I'll be able to get us away from here, if that's what you want. I'll do anything you wanna do just as long as I have you right by my side."

She smiled warmly, then reached out and took ahold of my face with her left hand. "You really do care about me, don't you?"

I slowly nodded my head. "Yeah, I really do, and I'll do anything for you. I feel like I'll be the one who gives you the world. I just gotta figure out how to go out and get it because I know you deserve it. You're the most beautiful girl I have ever seen before. I'm already crazy about you, and I just want to make and keep you happy for as long as I'm alive." I turned my head to the side and kissed the palm of her hand, then allowed her to continue holding my face.

We sat there for what seemed like ten minutes staring at one another, then she leaned in and I felt my heartbeat quicken. I leaned forward and closed my eyes, anticipating the feel of her juicy lips. I felt like I couldn't breathe as we moved in closer and closer, and then we connected, my lips over hers and hers on mine. First a peck, searching, then with more passion and aggression. She took a deep breath and exhaled into my mouth, moaning a little bit, just enough to drive me crazy. I pulled her more to me, wrapping my arms around her possessively, so much so we wound up mostly in the passenger's seat, both breathing hard and with my heart pounding so forcefully in my chest it hurt.

Finally she broke the kiss, sat back in her seat, and held two fingers to her lips, shaking her head. "I'm so sorry. I shouldn't have went that hard already. I just needed to kiss you so bad. It's so hard to explain." She lowered her head and ran her tongue over her lips, real sexy-like. After she was done, they were shinin' and I was having a hard time because she had me feeling some type of way.

I grabbed her hand and kissed the palm once again. "You didn't do nothin' wrong. I wanted to kiss you just as bad." I exhaled loudly. "I know it may not seem like it, but just as bad as you feel like you need me, I need you just as much. I am broken." I looked into her pretty face and she smiled, so I leaned forward and kissed her juicy lips once again, already addicted to their feel. We swapped spit for another two minutes.

She broke the kiss and laughed. "Well, go ahead and handle whatever you gotta take care of with your brother, but meet me back here tonight. I need you. I don't know how we're going to make it out of Jersey, but I want out of here. This city is full of heartache and pain for me. I'd be willing to go anywhere with you for a fresh start. I don't even care about going to our graduation anymore because I'm pretty sure my mother and sister won't be there to support me." I could hear her voice starting to break up again, and now it was affecting me ten times worse than before. I didn't like seeing her hurting.

I was willing to do absolutely anything I could to make her feel better. "Okay, well, I promise I'll be back as soon as I can, huh. Put your number into my phone and I'll be able to let you know what's good from time to time." I handed her my phone and she grabbed it, then wrapped her arms around the top of my neck, not saying a word, just holding me.

Jelissa

Chapter 8

Idris "Shotgun" Wright

I sat behind the wheel of the 2019 police-issued, black-on-black Dodge Charger with a shotgun on my lap. My rookie partner, Sheldon, was in the passenger's seat, and three other patrol cars were parked behind us, ready to execute one of the biggest drug busts of my legit career. And instead of me being one hundred percent focused, especially since I was running point on this operation, the one thing dominating all my thoughts was Leesee and the fact she'd left school early. I didn't know where she was or what she was doing, but every second I didn't know was a second I felt brought me closer to having a heart attack. I exhaled loudly and tried to get ahold of myself. Any second now I was going to give the order for the Yangs' internal electrical power to be shut off, then we were goin' to bum-rush them and hope to recover more than 80 kilos of pure Fentanyl.

Sheldon pulled his mask down over his face and cocked his automatic shotgun. "You a'ight over there, boss man? You look a li'l sick. Anything I can do to help?" he asked.

I looked over to him and shook my head. I never liked working with anybody. I preferred to be alone. I felt like partners were nothin' more than a loose end because I didn't play by the books. Never had, never would.

"I'm good, just mentally preparing myself for what comes next. I been working this case for nine months. It feels pretty surreal that it's coming to a close," I lied. I wasn't worried about what came next because, truth be told, I already had it figured out. I had a confidential informant on the inside who had already given me the blueprints to the interior of the house. We were set to recover no less than eighty kilos, though I wasn't willing to turn in more than forty. Those forty kilos I'd keep were valued at over three million dollars. Fentanyl was in heavy demand, and I intended to cash in off of it.

Hunter crept alongside my car and popped up slowly. "Boss, we're waiting for the order. You ready?" he asked with the winter smoke wafting from his mouth.

I nodded. "Yeah, let's go. Hit the lights."

I watched him hold up a hand and turn it in a circle, then wave forward. All of the patrol cars emptied out and headed to the house with a battering ram. I jumped out of my car and jogged over beside my comrades as we made our way through the blizzard. I climbed the porch, positioned right behind Hunter. He took the battering ram, pulled it backward, then with one swoosh through the air, *whoom!* He crashed it into the door, knocking it in, and I ran inside with my shotgun raised on bidness.

"Freeze! Newark P.D.!" I hollered, staying low to the ground.

I saw three Asian men on the couch. As we crashed through the door, they threw their hands in the air. In front of them was a table full of money and a counting machine beside it.

I eyed the cash closely, seeing that it was nothing but fifties and hundreds. I wished I'd hit them alone because that money would have never made it into evidence, but I shook my head and made my way into the next room, staying as low to the ground as possible. Two officers out in front of me kicked in a door to the left and one to the right, and that's when the gunfire erupted from both sides, causing me to drop to the floor on my stomach.

Boom! Boom! Boom!

"Ah! I'm hit! I'm hit!" one of the officers screamed as the rapid gunfire sounded from the bedroom to my right. He flew against the wall to the side of me and fell to his ass. His assault rifle flew across the carpet.

More shots rang out. I low-crawled backward, trying my best to get out of harm's way as the other officers jumped over me and headed to the action, screaming for the suspect to freeze and drop his weapon. More chaos and gunfire erupted as more officers poured into that vicinity.

I made my way to the back of the house with Hunter at my side. "You ready?" he hollered with his back to the wall on the side of the master bedroom door.

I nodded, then jumped up and kicked in the door as hard as I could before falling to the carpet on my stomach. See, it had already been arranged that our confidential informant would be in this room with the safe already open. Me and Hunter were supposed to rush in and supposedly catch him in the act of closing it, but before he could we would arrest him and give him a deal to roll over on a few of the heads of his organization. But we had other plans.

I fell to my stomach and Hunter rushed in with his shotgun raised. Just as planned, Voo Yang was on his knees with the big safe wide open, trying to push the kilos back into it. Hunter rushed him at full speed, and as soon as he got close enough he slammed the barrel of his shotgun into Voo Yang's forehead. I jumped up and let off two quick shots. *Boom. Boom*, hitting the man once in the neck and once in the chest before taking out a dirty .45 and shooting up the door and wall behind us after wrapping Voo Yang's hand around the pistol.

Hunter got up and stepped out of the room, closing the door behind him as more chaos ensued throughout the house. I knelt down and looked into the big safe, eyeing the packages of Fentanyl. I knew it was going to be difficult to get all of them out and into my trunk, but me and Hunter had been down this road before. I was running point on this operation, and he was second in command. After everything wound down, we'd be able to appoint our men where we needed them to go. Then we'd split our take fifty-fifty.

After it was all said and done, I didn't make my way home until three in the morning. I was exhausted and heavily worn out. In my black duffle bag were twenty kilos of Fentanyl and fifteen thousand dollars in cash. All in all a nice lick, but I wasn't happy because all I could think about was Leesee. My body yearned for hers. I missed her scent and the way she felt in my arms.

She reminded me so much of her mother when she was her age. Back then she'd broken my heart into a million pieces, going back and forth between me and Rah'nell, and for the most part choosing him. Playing with my emotions so much it drove me crazy. I thought about her every second of the day, and whenever I saw them together it made me sick to my stomach. So sick I knew I had to get rid of him, one way or the other.

And though it took me some time, I finally made it happen: a setup for a murder I knew he'd never be able to come from under. With him out of the picture, I set my sights on the most purest form of Deidre in this world: the little perfect Leesee. The only one who could heal those old wounds from the past. A finer version of the one who hurt me, but the same blood and makeup. I was obsessed with her, and I needed her just to make sense of my life.

I found myself shakin' like crazy as I entered into the house, especially after not seeing her car parked in front of it. "Baby! Baby, where you at?" I hollered, setting the duffle bag on the floor and my service weapon on the couch in the living room.

Deidre turned on the light in the hallway, and made her way down it, dressed in a see-through purple Victoria's Secret number that usually drove me crazy. From a distance I could almost imagine she was Leesee, though her body was a little more mature in width.

"Hey, baby. I been waiting up for you all night," she said, closing the distance between us. She came and wrapped her arms around my waist. "I missed you, baby."

I removed her arms and looked down on her. "Did she come home yet?" I was in a frenzy, worried about the only person who meant anything to me in life. It felt like nails were being scratched on a chalkboard all around me. I was becoming hysterical. I needed her so bad.

Deidre knocked my hands away and took a step back. "Did who come home yet?" she asked nastily.

Love Me Even When It Hurts

I grabbed both of her shoulders and slammed her into the wall so quick I couldn't even believe I did it until it was already done. "Don't play wit' me. You know who I'm talking about. Did Leesee come home yet?" I dug my nails into her shoulder as I felt myself getting more and more angry. I could barely think straight. I kept imagining her soft lips and pretty eyes, the feel of her soft skin against mine and her deep moans, her faces of passion. I needed my baby girl. I needed her like never before.

Deidre pushed me away. "Get the fuck off of me! You son of a bitch!" She blinked tears. "Here I am waiting up for you all night, and the first thing you do as soon as you come into the house is inquire about her? What type of shit is that, Idris? What about me? Don't you care about me anymore? Don't I –"

Smack! I backhanded her so hard she fell against the wall, then I pulled her up by her hair and smacked her again, this time raising my hand high in the air to ensure I made crazy impact. I wasn't playing about my baby girl, and I felt like this bitch was hiding something from me. I flung her to the ground and got on top of her, wrapping my right hand around her neck and squeezing. "Bitch, don't nobody in this world mean more to me than Leesee. That's my muthafuckin' baby girl, and I need her now, so you betta tell me where the fuck she at or I'ma kill you right here and right now on this muthafuckin' floor." To emphasize my point, I wrapped both hands around her neck and squeezed tightly while she kicked her legs in the air. I started to imagine another nigga putting his hands on my baby, touching her in the ways only I should have. I saw her face of passion and imagined her forgetting about me because of some other man, and I couldn't take it.

I felt my throat get tight, and then I was clenching my teeth, squeezing Deidre's neck harder and harder. "Tell me, bitch! Where is my daughter?"

She humped up into me, trying to buck me off, but wasn't nothing happening. I was finna kill this bitch because I felt like it was her fault Leesee had run away. I knew it didn't have shit to do wit' me. She loved me. Her mother was just in the way, so if I killed her, we would be able to be together happily ever after.

I squeezed harder and she stopped kicking, just lay flat, gagging.

"Daddy! Please! You're killing her!" Nia screamed as she opened her bedroom door and ran down the hallway at full speed before dropping to her knees beside us, trying to get me to release my hands from around her neck. "Please don't kill her, Daddy! Please!" she begged with tears running down her cheeks.

I shook my head from right to left. "It's her fault, Nia. It's her fault that Leesee gone. She made my daughter leave me. She made her hate me, Nia. I can't let that shit ride. I just can't." I squeezed harder as Nia got up from the floor and disappeared down the hallway.

Underneath me Deidre was lying flat on her back with her hands at her sides. Her eyes were closed and there was no more fight in her, yet I continued to squeeze as if my life depended on it.

Bam! *Tish*! Something crashed into the back of my head ,causing me to fall off her and onto my stomach. I could feel my blood running down the back of my neck and into my shirt. I struggled to get up, but felt so woozy.

"I'm your fuckin' daughter, not her! I don't know why you hate us so much, but it's not fair!" Nia screamed before slamming whatever she was using into the back of my head again.

I fell flat to my stomach and felt paralyzed. I watched her lean over her mother and place her ear to her chest.

Her eyes grew wide and she screamed out loud. "No! Mommy! Please! No!" She opened Deidre's mouth and began to blow into it, then clasped her fingers together, placing them on her chest and doing CPR, going back and forth between giving her air and the chest compressions. "Breathe, Mommy! Please breathe," she begged.

Slowly, I came out of my fog and started to regain my senses. I slowly made my way to a sitting position before staggering to my feet while Nia continued to try to bring

Love Me Even When It Hurts

Deidre back to life. Just as I saw Deidre's feet kick out, I reached down and grabbed a handful of Nia's hair and yanked her head backward so hard I heard her neck snap. "Bitch, where is my baby girl? Where the fuck did your mother send her off to? I need her, and I need her now!" I hollered, feeling dizzy.

Nia screamed at the top of her lungs and ran backward into me, making me crash into the wall and release her. Once released, she ran into the kitchen, and I could hear the kitchen drawer open up. Then she reappeared with a knife in her hand.

"I'm tired of this shit, Daddy. I'm not going to let you hurt either one of us anymore. Now leave. Please leave, Daddy, or I'm going to kill you, and I don't want to do that because I love you so much. You're my only father, but you're sick in the head. You need help," she cried walking closer to me.

I reached down and grabbed Deidre's free right hand and dragged her closer to me. "Tell me where my baby girl is or I'm going to kill yo' mama. Now tell me, bitch! Now! And don't ever call me yo' daddy again. I only got one daughter! She's perfect, and she ain't you! Now, where is she?"

I dropped to my knees and began to choke Deidre again, and that's when Nia ran full-speed down the hall with the knife in her hand As soon as she got close enough, I dove and rolled under her ass, causing her to trip and fall. It was an old trick they'd taught us back in the police academy to catch a perpetrator off guard.

She fell onto her stomach, and the knife flew across the hardwood floor. I jumped up, ran over to her, and wrapped her neck in my forearm while I sat on her back. "Where is my daughter, bitch? I ain't gon' ask you again." I loosened my grip just enough for her to give me an answer.

"Grandma's, Daddy. She staying there for a few days. Please, let me go. Ack! Ack!"

I was so mad I wasn't thinking clearly. I hated both of them for making my baby girl want to leave the house.

Jelissa

I hated them for teaming up on her, which is what I assumed they'd done. I would make them pay. I would get rid of them so I could have my baby all to myself. I needed her like nobody understood, needed her worse than ever. I felt like I had not had her in years.

I tightened my grip and proceeded to choke Nia with everything I had. I had to kill her. I had to get rid of her so Leesee would know she was the only daughter I needed, that I would never allow anybody to stand in the way of our love.

It took less than five minutes for me to take Nia's life, then I finished Deidre in the same fashion before wrapping them up in plastic and placing them one-by-one into the trunk of my car. I knew just where to dispose of their bodies.

After I finished, I was on a mission to find my baby girl by any means.

Chapter 9

Rome

"So that's how this muthafucka gon' flow right here. Pretty much all you gotta do is let li'l homie, me, an' them answer the door while you lay back in the cut with this banger. Anything seem fishy, you don't hesitate to empty this clip in a nigga's ass. You understand me?" Kazi said, handing me a .44 Desert Eagle off his waist.

He'd been lacing me all night, ever since I'd left Leesee's side, giving me the ins and outs on the two trap houses he wanted me to run on Mulberry Drive. I really didn't have to do much because he had some li'l young hustlers in each trap wit' me that handled the dope addicts. All I had to do was take the bread from them, keep my eye on the supply of heroin, and make sure everything ran smoothly. He was giving me a salary of three gees a week and ten percent of whatever we brought in every day, which I thought was cool. To get me started he'd already given me two gees and the pistol.

"Yeah, I understand you perfectly fine, and I got this, so don't even trip. I need this money. I won't fuck up, you got my word on that." I put the gun on my waist and sat down at the table, sealing the two Ziploc bags of heroin and stuffing them into the big hole in the back of the couch before pushing it back against the wall. "What time li'l homie an' them supposed to shut down for the night?" I asked, looking over to Kazi as he handed each teen about five hunnit apiece.

He shrugged his shoulders. "That's all up to you. You getting ten percent of everything they bring in, so if it was me I'd have they li'l asses hustling until they passed out, let 'em rest for a few hours, then open shop right back out. Time is money, and the more time they spend rocking this bitch, that's more money in each of our pockets. Besides, where do you have to go?" he asked, stuffing a bundle of cash into his left front pocket after putting a rubber band around it.

I got up and walked over closer to him, looking over my shoulder at the two li'l dudes as they played the PlayStation, lost in the television screen. My brother gave me a look like I'd lost my mind the closer I got to him.

"Bruh, let me holler at you back here for a minute, if you don't mind," I said, walking into the back room with him following me.

As soon as he stepped in, he nodded his head upward. "What's good?"

I took a deep breath and exhaled. "I gotta go get Leesee, man. Right now she going through something, and I just need to be there for her as much as I can."

He frowned. "That girl from next door?"

I nodded. "Yeah, bruh. Let me go snatch her up real quick and bring her back here. Probably let her get some sleep in the room across the hall. It got a bed in there, right?" I asked, trying to recall if I saw one in there or not.

Kazi faced me with a mug on his face. "Bruh, what's good wit' you and that li'l bitch? She ain't on shit? She ain't even got no money, so she can't benefit you in no way at all. That's another thing you gon' learn about this game: it's pointless to fuck wit' anybody that can't benefit you in one way or the other. Nigga, you gon' lose a lot of money chasing pussy, but you'll never lose no pussy chasing money, you feel me? So fuck that li'l bitch. I got plenty project hoez that's gon' swallow yo' shit, then ride you until you pass out. Shorty a rookie, I can tell. Plus she got that Shotgun nigga all up her ass and shit. That nigga kiss her on her lips and everything, and that's weird, seeing as that's his daughter and all."

"Step-daughter. They ain't blood. He just fuck wit' her mother and look at her as a daughter figure," I said, feeling myself become heated. I felt like my brother was purposely disrespecting her for no reason, and that shit was pissing me off.

He waved me off. "Whatever. No matter what, that shit weird, and I don't think you should be fuckin' wit' her 'cause she ain't gon' do nothin' but bring drama our way. I'd hate to have to smoke Shotgun over yo' bitch when it's all this pussy out here."

I lowered my head and flared my nostrils. "Bro, word is bond, stop calling her out her name. That shit ain't cool."

He jerked his head back. "What? Man, fuck that bitch. I call every female the same thing, including Mama when she piss me off. You think I'ma make an exception for that ho next door?" He sucked his teeth. "Nigga, please."

I stepped into his face, fuming. My vision was hazy, and I saw myself blowing his head off over his utter disrespect for Leesee. "Nigga, I don't care what you call them other females, she ain't got nothin' to do wit' that. But I ain't finna honor you calling her out her name. Not in front of me. I ain't going." I clenched my jaw and looked up at him, ready for whatever.

Kazi too a step back and looked me up and down. "Oh shit, li'l nigga, you care about her like that? I mean, already? Since when?" he asked with a smirk on his face.

I shook my head. "That shit don't even matter. The fact is I do. She been through a lot, and it's on me to hold her down and heal her now. I know how it feels to be in this cold world and nobody cares about you, but I'm a dude. I can handle it. She's a female, so I know it gotta be ten times worse for them, especially when the people who are hurting you the most are the ones who live in the same house wit' you."

Kazi snickered at that. "Oh yeah, so tell me what you finna do to help her? 'Cause you ain't got shit, and if I don't help, you ain't gon' be shit. Nigga, both of y'all losing." He curled his upper lip. "Matter fact, get the fuck out my trap, nigga, since you wanna act so tough. Go run to that bitch and tell her to put yo' bum ass on. I wash my hands of you. Beat it! Now!" He pulled out two .40 Glocks, cocking first one, and then the other.

Before I could gather myself, I looked behind me to see the two li'l dudes he wanted to hustle under me were standing at the end of the hallway with revolvers in their hands and mugs on their faces.

"What's good, boss?" the dark-skinned, fat one asked.

Kazi raised his guns into my face. "Shit, just making this fuck-nigga get out my trap. He better hope it stopped snowing, or else shit gon' be real ugly for 'em tonight, cuz."

I looked Kazi in the eye and nodded my head. "That's alright, nigga. But one day you gon' need me. One day you gon' wish you treated me better than you have. I'ma figure life out, and no matter what, I'm riding beside Leesee until my last breath, so call me what you want."

"Nigga, get yo' Captain Save-A-Ho ass out my trap before I have my li'l niggaz stank you. Word is bond, we ain't cut from the same cloth." He shook his head. "That nigga Shotgun gon' kill yo' stupid ass for fuckin' wit' his daughter. Just watch. You ain't nothin' but a dead man walking."

Those were the last words I heard before I made my way out into the cold. Luckily for me the snow had stopped coming down, though the streets were horrible. There were a few plow trucks out getting started, but I had a hard time keeping the Jeep from sliding all over the road. I texted Leesee and told her I was on my way, but didn't make it to her grandmother's house until two hours later by the grace of God.

When I got there, she was already on her way down the stairs. I opened her passenger door and she got in, throwing her arms around my neck. "Baby, I didn't think you were going to come back. I thought you were going to abandon me. I was so worried," she cried with her face in the crux of my neck.

I shook my head. "Never that. I told you it's my job to hold you down, so I got you with everything I am for the rest of my life. I promise." I held her more firmly, then moved her long curly hair out of her face and kissed her soft lips, being as gentle as I possibly could, but Lord knows I needed her so bad.

Love Me Even When It Hurts

"Baby, you gotta take me to my mother's house. I think somethin' is wrong. My sister texted me and said Idris had lost his mind. I don't know what that means, but when I asked her what was going on she didn't respond. And even though we're on rocky terms, she'd never leave me in limbo like that, especially after reaching out to me first, so I'm worried. Do you think we can make it out there to them with the roads the way they are?"

She rubbed the side of my face and looked deep into my gray eyes, sending chills throughout my body. I already knew I would do anything for her. I mean, I don't know why she had such a hold on me, but she absolutely did.

"Baby, I'll do whatever you want me to do. Come on, let's make it happen," I said, starting the ignition and pulling slowly away from the curb.

***

Shotgun

I poured the gasoline on both bodies that lay inside of the big, metal garbage can before taking a match and setting them ablaze. I watched the flames shoot high into the warehouse. I knew on average it would take about thirty minutes for the skin to start melting off of the bones. After that was concluded, I'd take the bones and smash them into dust, then bury them in the woods. *But the burning comes first*, I thought as I added more fluid to the fire.

Two hours of doing this and I was sure I was going to get the result I was looking for. After the flames died out, I fanned away the smoke as the heavy, putrid scent of charred human flesh attacked my nose. Looking into the garbage can, I could see two blackened skeletons. I smiled at that as my phone buzzed. I answered it right away.

"Hello, who is this?" I asked, closing the top of the garbage can.

"Idris, this is William. I just want to let you know that my granddaughter is here, and she's crying a lot. I think something is wrong. You should get over here as soon as you can," he said before coughing up a storm.

"William? William, who is you talking about?" I asked, already jogging back to my car and getting in. I was praying he was talking about Leesee, but I knew for a fact the man had about ten grandchildren by marriage, so I couldn't be too sure. I started the ignition and backed my car all the way out of the snowy lot, skidding across the snow before the car came to a halt.

"I'm talking about Leesee. She's downstairs with her grandmother with all that damn crying that's driving me crazy. Get yo' ass over here and get this girl before I put her out. It's too early in the morning for all that shit. I gotta get up at the crack of dawn and go to work. Now hurry up!"

I felt myself shaking the whole way there. I was only about fifteen minutes away, but with the snow being as heavy as it was, it would delay me by about an additional ten minutes. But I didn't care. I flipped on my sirens and stepped on the gas, throwing all caution to the wind. I needed my baby girl. I had to get her back in my arms and back into the sheets where her body was the only one that could heal me. The whole way I kept on saying her name out loud. Every time I uttered it, it made me harder and harder. I missed her scent badly. I missed the way she felt on the inside. I needed to hear her call me Daddy. I needed to tie her up and do all of the things to her body I knew she needed done to it. She belonged to me. She was my property, and I would make her understand it as soon as I got her back. She'd never try that running shit again.

I pulled up into the back of her grandmother's house shortly thereafter, jumped out, and ran through the snow until I got to the back door. Once there, I started to beat on it like a mad man. "William! William! I'm here, man. Open up," I hollered, looking around. The sun had not begun to rise. It was pitch dark in the backyard, the only light coming from the back of a house about six gates over.

Love Me Even When It Hurts

William appeared a few minutes later with an angry look on his face. He slung the door open and upped a .357 Magnum, pointing it at my chest. "Get in here, you sick son of a bitch."

I curled my upper lip and lowered my eyes into slits, putting my hands up. "What is this all about, William?" I sized him up quickly. I knew I could move on him and take the gun away, but I didn't want to make a mistake and have it go off, waking the neighbors. I knew they stayed in a community of older, nosey residents. I didn't need the police being called before I could get my daughter back. There were so many things I hadn't finished just yet, too many loose ends, so I allowed myself to be apprehended.

He pulled me into the house roughly, taking me to the basement where there was a chair for me to sit in. He slammed me down into it and took a step back. His big body looking as if it weighed no less than three hundred pounds, his beard as long as Santa Clause's.

I eyed him with hatred, knowing I was going to kill him and whoever else was in the house. I wanted my daughter, and nobody was going to stand in the way of me gettin' her back. "What's this all about?" I asked again.

"Martha! Martha! Baby, I got him! Come on down, it's okay. If he move, I'm gon' blow his head off. Bring the tape recorder!" he hollered, looking in the direction of the stairs.

Tape recorder? I thought. What the fuck did they think they were finna do with that?"

William lowered his eyes into slits. "Son, I knows yo' daddy, and I know yo' whole family struggles wit' that bi-polar disorder. Deidre say you ain't been taking yo' meds. Is that the reason you did what you did to my granddaughter?" he asked, then threw his hand up. "Wait, don't answer, let Martha get down here so we can record it." He looked back toward the stairs with a scowl on his face. "Hurry yo' li'l self up now, woman. I ain't got all day."

Slowly, but surely, Martha made her way down the last few steps and went all the way around until she was standing behind him. "Well, you know I just got my hips replaced. How you expect me to move like I'm twenty one when I ain't move that way since I was sixteen?" She shook her head, looked down at the tape recorder, and started it. "Did he say why he been taking advantage of Leesee yet?" she asked, looking up to him.

He shook his head. "Sho' ain't, but we 'bout to get to the bottom of this right now. You see, he's the police. The only way we gon' be able to get any form of justice is if we get it all on this here tape recorder. They some of the dirtiest bastards in the country. Needless to say, I never liked you, Idris. Knew you was dirty, just like yo' no-good daddy. Now, why you been assaulting Leesee? Have you been off yo' medication for that long?"

I felt my shoulders jerk out of nowhere at the mention of my medications. It was true I'd stopped taking my medications a long time ago. At one point in time I just didn't feel like I needed them, felt like I could function all on my own even though I was diagnosed with severe bipolar disorder when I was only nine years old. Then, at ten, they diagnosed me with schizophrenia. I didn't like nobody telling me I was nuts or I couldn't function without them pumping man-made poison into my system. I was stronger than that. I didn't need anybody's meds, and the fact William was bringing up my family's history was pissing me off.

I attempted to stand up and get into his face. I wanted to let him know exactly how I felt after I snapped his neck.

He took a step forward and frowned. "If you don't sit yo' ass back in that chair, I'm gon' send you to your father Lucifer and pray about it this Sunday. Sit yo' ass down! Now!" he ordered.

I mugged him for a long time, then took my seat. I could hear Leesee's voice calling out to me, screaming that she needed me, that her grandparents were trying to keep her away from me. I felt my heartbeats speed up. I started to miss and need her real bad. The room seemed to spin and tilt all around me. I needed my baby girl.

94

Love Me Even When It Hurts

"Where the fuck is my daughter, William?" I hollered, feeling my blood boil.

Martha stepped forward with the tape recorder. "You hurt her, Idris. That girl say you been hurting her ever since she was twelve years old, but lately you've been heartless. What's the matter with you? Don't you know that ain't right?" she asked, stepping a little closer to me.

I shook my head. "I would never hurt my baby girl. I love her with all my heart. She belongs to me. I could never harm someone so precious to my soul." I heard Leesee's voice screaming out to me. It sounded like she was close, somewhere in the house. The room began to tilt even more, causing me to become dizzy.

"You hurt her, Idris! She sat here and told my wife everything, and she never wants to see you again. You're going to jail if I have anything to do with it. Now, admit what you did! Say it out loud so we can get you some help!" he grumbled.

The only thing I heard him say clearly was she didn't want to see me again, and I knew that was a lie. It was just like Leesee was screaming at me: all they wanted to do was keep her away from me, and I wasn't going to allow that. No way, no how. I knew what I had to do in order to get out of the position I was in so I could get back to my baby girl, and I was going to do it to the best of my ability.

Jelissa

Chapter 10

Leesee

I jiggled my key into the lock, turned it, and pushed the door inward. "Nia! Nia! Are you home? Where are you, li'l sis?" I hollered, rushing into the house with Rome right behind me. I was in such a rush to get into the house I wound up tripping over the big, black duffle bag in the middle of the living room floor. Luckily, I caught myself and wound up in a push-up position.

Rome leaned down and picked me up as if I only weighed a pound, placing me back on my feet. "You okay, baby?" he asked, looking me over carefully, then taking his thumb and rubbing my cheek with it.

"Yeah, I'm good. I'm just clumsy." I dusted myself off, looked into his sexy gray eyes for a minute, and had to shake my head to snap out of the zone they were placing me in. I turned away from him and looked down the hallway. "It don't seem like nobody is here, which is odd because my mother's car is in the driveway. Maybe she's just ignoring me or asleep or somethin'. I know this bag belongs to Idris because I've seen him with it on more than one occasion. It feels heavy, though. You check and see what's in there, and I'll go see if my mother's in her room and just ignoring me." I hugged him and broke our embrace. I didn't care if he looked through Idris' things because I wasn't planning on seeing the man ever again.

I turned the light on in the hallway as Rome took the big bag and placed it on the couch behind me, preparing to unzip it. As soon as I turned on the light, for some reason I felt a little scared, like something was going to jump out at me. I just had this eerie feeling walking down that hallway.

The first door I came to was my sister's. She had a sign on it that said 'knock before you enter,' which is what I did. I knocked on it three times and waited for her to answer me. "Nia. Nia, open up, it's me. Please don't be ignoring me. I really need to speak to you. I'm worried," I whimpered. I waited a few more seconds, then twisted the knob and pushed the door in, walking slowly into her room after switching the light on. Her bed was fully made up, and on top of it was a new Fendi outfit she'd bought only two weeks back. On her nightstand was her cell phone. I walked over to it, picked it up, and saw there were ten missed calls. Six of them were from me, and the other four were from Jamal's punk-ass. I wondered if she even knew what had transpired between us two, or maybe she knew and just didn't care.

I put her phone back on the night table and made my way out of her room, down the hallway, and to my mother's door, which was also closed. I put my ear against it and could hear the sounds of R. Kelly playing out of the speakers in her room. I had to build up the nerve to actually knock on her door. I was so worried about her opening it and kicking my ass because she had already said she never wanted us to speak to one another again. I didn't know if she really meant it, but a part of me felt like she did.

"Mama? Mama, are you in there?" I asked knocking lightly on her door. "I know you said we aren't supposed to talk to each other ever again, but I just need to know you're safe and sound. I'm so worried about you. Please answer me." I knocked three more times and tried her doorknob, finding it turned. I pushed the door inward and saw inside her room it was dimly lit. There was a silver bucket with a bottle of champagne floating in water. Beside that was what looked like two rolled joints and an ashtray. I knew my mother and Idris smoked weed at times, and it never bothered me because it was the only drug I'd ever seen my mother do.

The covers on her bed were pulled back, and on top of them was a pair of freshly folded boxers, a black wife beater, and some cologne. That puzzled me a little bit, but I simply shrugged my shoulders at it. What had me confused the most was the fact my mother was nowhere in sight.

Love Me Even When It Hurts

I looked to my right and saw her bathroom door was closed, but underneath it was a puddle of water. My eyes grew as big as saucers. The first thing I thought about was her being drowned in the tub, so I nearly broke my neck rushing to the door, turning the knob, and pushing it inward.

I was met by a rush of water. The bathroom was completely flooded. Up ahead, the tub was full and both faucets were going. Something wasn't right.

"Baby!" Rome hollered, appearing in the doorway and scaring the living daylights out of me. My heart damn near jumped out of my chest. I had to lean against the wall to keep from falling down because my knees were so weak.

I walked into the bathroom, into all of the water, and turned off the faucets. "What's the matter, Rome?" I yelled.

"You need to see this. I think it's some blood on the carpet in the hallway, and the kitchen is messed up. It looks like somebody was looking for somethin'."

The next thing I knew I found myself knelt down in the middle of the hallway, touching five different stains on the floor that looked like blood. I didn't know what had taken place before we got there, but I was feeling sick to my stomach. I just felt like something wasn't right.

I didn't even know I was shaking so bad until I felt Rome's arms wrapping around me. "Baby, are you okay? I'm here for you, however you need me to be," he said softly.

I shook my head. "It's Idris. I just know it is. He's done something to my mother and Nia. He's out of his mind, and when he is, he does things that are just ridiculous. Do you think that's really blood?" I asked, hoping he would say no.

He took a deep breath. "Yeah, it is, baby. And it's a lot of it, too. Somebody hurt. The kitchen messed up real bad, and did you miss that lamp at the end of the hall?" he said, pointing.

Jelissa

I snapped my head in its direction and noticed it for the first time. The lamp my mother usually kept in her living room, the big white one, was shattered into pieces. I slapped my hands to my face in disbelief. It was right outside of the main bathroom in the hallway. I don't know how I missed it. "No, I didn't see that. What do you think it means?" I asked, trembling worse than ever. I was scared out of my mind and worried for my sister and mother.

Rome tightened his arms around me. "Look, I don't know what's going on, but we gotta get out of here before dude get back. Something tells me this got Shotgun written all over it. We need to get to a safe place, then call around to see if your people are at any of your relatives' houses."

I lowered my head. "He always said if I ever left him, he would kill everybody and then me. I'm so scared, Rome. We can't even call the police because he is one. So what do we do?" I wrapped my arms around him and hugged with all I had. I needed him ten times more now. I was so afraid he would leave my side, leave me alone to face the monster that was Idris.

I knew he was going to kill me. I knew he would never allow me to be away from him for long without coming after me. The world seemed to close in on me. It seemed like I was under a dark cloud, that at any minute Idris would appear to take my life. I was so scared I didn't want to let Rome's arm go.

He got onto his knees and faced me, wrapping me protectively in his big arms. "Look, baby, I promise I'm not gon' let nothin' happen to you. I will protect you with everything I am as a man. You have my word on that." He kissed me on the forehead and then the lips before brushing my hair out of my face. "You are my angel, and there is nothin' I won't do for you. But come on, we gotta get out of here, and fast." He pulled me up and wiped away my tears. "You know I got you, right?"

I looked into his piercing gray eyes, and felt like this man would never allow Idris to get to me. For some reason those gray things spoke to my heart and my soul all at once. Within them I felt and saw my security. "Yes, I do. I trust you, Rome, and even though I know you may not believe me just yet, I just wanna let you know I love you, and I'm going to do my all to be everything it is you see in me. I need you so bad." I hugged him tightly as he kissed my forehead.

"Come on, baby, let's bounce." He pulled my hand and took me back to the front of the house, where he leaned down and picked up the duffle bag. "Yo, I don't know where he got this stuff from, but its like twenty kilos in here and at least twenty gees. I mean, I won't take it if you don't want me to, but I think we should. Ain't no telling how it's gon' come in handy."

I shrugged my shoulders. "Baby, I'm following you. However you want to lead, I'll follow. I'm so lost right now that I don't know what to do."

He put the duffle bag on his shoulder and nodded. "I got us, boo, trust me. I got this. Let's run to my house real quick so I can make sure my mother straight. Once that's confirmed, we off into the night. We gotta figure this world out together, just me and you until the end. You wit' me?"

I stood on my tippy-toes and kissed his cheek. "I'm wit' you, baby. I'm wit' you until the bitter end." And as negative as it may sound, I figured bitter was exactly how our end was going to be.

***

Shotgun

"So yeah, I been tripping ever since I been off of my medication, and I'm man enough to say I need help. I would have never done those things to Leesee had I been in my right state of mind. You gotta believe me. I love her and my girls with all of my heart, Martha," I said with tears running down my cheeks.

Jelissa

One whole hour later and her old ass was still recording everything coming out of my mouth while her punk-ass husband held me at gunpoint. I'd given them all of the shit I figured they wanted to hear, all the while I could hear Leesee's voice screaming from the walls, telling me they only wanted to keep us apart, that I needed to get rid of them. That if I got rid of them, then we could be together happily ever after and nobody would try to break us apart again.

Martha shook her head in disgust. "Po' chil'. I knew you was struggling with that there disorder. Deidre used to tell me how bad you had it when you'd missed more than one day without taking your meds. That's sad," she sighed. "Well, William, I think we got enough to go to the police. Sho' hope so. This here chil' needs professional help and Jesus. They'll figure it out, though. I'll be right back. Gonna go make that call." She patted him on the shoulder, lowered her head, and made her way up the stairs.

William yawned. "Well, hurry up. I'm ready to get this shit over wit'. I done missed a whole night's rest, plus my arm starting to hurt. Tell them police to come and do their job."

As soon as she left, I looked at him from the corner of my eye. He was about six feet away from me. I was tired of sitting in one place, and I damn sure wasn't about to let that bitch make that call. I rolled my head around on my shoulders. "William, you really ready to kill me, huh?" I asked, feeling my adrenalin coursin' through me. Martha had only been gone for about thirty seconds. I knew my window was small. My heart started to beat faster and faster.

He yawned again, placing his hand over his mouth. "Boy, what are you talking about? I'm hoping nobody gotta die today. You just sit still and everythang will be taken care of shortly."

I stood up. "I gotta piss, and I'm not about to sit here and pee on myself, so if you gon' kill me, then go ahead and do it." In my head Martha had been gone for about

102

Love Me Even When It Hurts

ninety seconds now, more than enough time to call the authorities.

William raised the gun and leveled it at me. "Boy, you betta sit yo' black ass back in that seat. Now, I don't wanna kill you, but I will. I swear I will." He stepped forward, and I was so happy he did, because now he was in arm's reach.

I threw my hands in the air and took a step toward him. "Really? You gon' kill me because I gotta piss? What type of shit is that?" I asked, taking one more step forward.

The old man was cocky. "If you don't sit yo' black ass down, I'm gon' –"

Before he could finish that sentence, I dropped to the ground and swept my leg under his, causing him to fall backward. He raised the gun in the air and let off a shot. *Boom!*

I didn't give a fuck. The screaming of Leesee's voice started to drive me crazy. I rushed him on my knees and wound up on top of him, wrestling for the gun as Martha made her way down the stairs.

"William? William? Please tell me you didn't kill him, baby? Please," she hollered, falling down the steps in a hurry to see what was going on. She must've really loved her husband, because I don't know anybody who would have run toward gunfire, but that's exactly what she did.

The old man was strong as a bull, and his grip was like that of a monkey. I shot my head forward and slammed my forehead into his face once, then two times in a row until he released the gun. As soon as it was out of his grasp, I took ahold of it, replaced the hammer, and turned it around, slamming it into his temple.

"No! No! You're killing him, Idris. Get off of my husband!" Martha screamed, jumping on my back.

As soon as she got on it, I flung her li'l round ass off of me before straddling her and beating her senseless with the same gun I had been pounding her husband with.

103

Jelissa

I didn't get to hit her more than twice before her husband was on his feet with blood gushing from his head. He staggered and picked up a pipe leaning against the washing machine before rushing toward me with it on wobbly legs. *Crack!* He hit me so hard across my back I hollered out in pain and rolled away from Martha.

"You evil son of a bitch. Get off of my wife. We ain't did nothing to you. Get on away from here now. Leave our home. Leesee ain't here," he spat with his eyes rolling into the back of his head.

I made my way to my feet and raised the gun. "Tell me where my daughter is. I hear her screaming for me. She's somewhere in this house, and she needs me. I'm the only one that can save her. So where is she? Tell me now!" I hollered. The room started to spin, and it seemed like William had morphed into two people, but I knew that couldn't be possible. It had to be my disorder getting the better of me, trying to take me down with the enemy. I couldn't let it prevail. My baby girl needed her daddy. I missed her so much.

William pulled Martha to her feet. The old lady was bleeding profusely with a big hole in her head. She squeezed her eyes tight and allowed her husband to wrap his arms around her protectively. "She left with that Rome boy that stays next to y'all house. She say she was going home to check on her mother and Nia. Please just go, Idris. Go find her and leave me and my husband alone. Your family is your family. We don't want anything else to do with it," she said sounding out of breath.

Leesee screamed my name and yelled that they had her locked up and were trying to kill her. She told me to get rid of them, to hurry, and if I didn't kill them they were going to keep her away from me forever. My vision got cloudy, then I saw Rome's face laughing in the distance. He was in collusion with Martha and William. He wanted to take my baby girl away from me as well. I had to kill him, but first the old people.

They had to go.

Love Me Even When It Hurts

I put my hands on my head to stop my brain from spinning so fast. I couldn't think clearly. All I could hear was Leesee's voice begging me to save her. Before I knew what I was doing, I rushed William at full speed. As soon as he saw me coming, he threw his wife behind him, raised the pole, and brought it down hard against my forearm with a loud clunk, but I was so amped up I barely felt any pain. I took the handle of his .357 and slammed it into the center of his forehead with all of my strength, then kneed him in the stomach and upper-cut him with a blow to the face. He flew to the side and landed against the water heater on one knee.

I rushed him again and slung the gun, cracking him in the side of the head, feeling the impact of the steel handle on his skull.

"Uh!" he hollered and fell to the concrete, shaking with blood coming out of his mouth.

"Kill 'im, Daddy. Kill 'im, Daddy. Kill 'im. He trying to keep me way from you! Hurry, Daddy. Get to me! Kill Martha, too! I need you!" Leesee screamed from somewhere inside the house.

I knelt down and continued to beat him over the head with the gun until he was unmoving, then I flipped him over and placed two fingers to his neck, checking for a pulse that wasn't there. My chest heaved up and down. The whole basement was the color of red. Everything looked fuzzy, and I had double vision.

I looked to see Martha slowly crawling toward the stairs on her elbows. Blood leaked out of her skull and dripped down the side of her face. "Uh! Uh! Help me, Father. Please. Please help me," she whimpered. She was on the third step, trying to pull herself upward.

"Don't let her get away, Daddy. She's trying to come and hurt me. She wants to keep me away from you. Get her! Kill her, Daddy! Now! Save me!" Leesee screamed.

"Ah!" I hollered, running full speed, grabbing Martha's legs and pulling her down the stairs before straddling her, placing my hands around her thick neck and squeezing like my life depended on it. "Die, bitch! Nobody can keep my daughter away from me. Nobody! Do you hear me?" I hollered, seeing the room flip upside down and spin 'round and 'round. The more it did, the harder I squeezed, feeling her fight against me.

Her blood oozed into the creases of my fingers. My heart pounded in my chest, making me struggle to breathe.

Chapter 11

Rome

I took the gun my brother had given me off my hip and sat it on my dresser, took off the sweaty wife-beater and threw it into the hamper before taking a soapy towel and hitting my armpits. I would do a better job when I got to the hotel later tonight, I thought. I was just a little insecure about the way I was smelling after I took my polo shirt off. I mean, it wasn't bad, but I didn't want Leesee to catch wind of it.

After I washed up as best I could, I threw on some deodorant and another Polo fit before grabbing my Marc Jacobs jacket and meeting Leesee in the living room where she sat on the couch with her head down. "Baby, I'm almost ready to go. Let me just ask my mother if she need anything.

She nodded her head. "Okay, honey."

As I was making my way to the back of the house, my mother met me halfway with a blank look on her face. "I don't know what you're up to, but don't bring that li'l girl in my house ever again. You gon' start a whole-ass war by fuckin' wit' that li'l bitch, I hope you know that." She turned around to walk away toward the kitchen with me following her.

I frowned. "Mama, what do you have against her? She's always been real respectful toward you," I asked, not understanding.

She walked to the sink and started to wash the few dished that were in there, pouring Ajax all over them. "Shotgun been fuckin' that girl for a long time, and he thinks she is Deidre. Just straight obsessed with her. You know he really crazy." She picked up a plate and began to wash it with the dishrag before setting it inside of the dish-washer.

I sighed. "She told me about all of that already, but that don't give you a reason to be mad at her. Dude been

Jelissa

taking her through a lot, and it ain't fair. I'm trying my best to help her move through it." I took the second plate out of her hand and placed it into the dishwasher.

"Well, I don't need all that drama in my house. I don't know why you think you can save that girl. Kazi told me you didn't even wanna hustle because you wanted to be all up her ass and shit. You old enough to get the fuck out of my house since you ain't bringing in no income. I tried to have your brother put you up on game, but it seem like you a lost cause, especially fucking with that li'l tramp in there." She pointed with her head while her hands were in the soapy water.

I was over it and had heard enough. I didn't know why my family insisted on disrespecting Leesee in the manner they did, but it made me angry immediately. My whole life I had never said anything disrespectful to my mother, but every time I heard her say something offensive about Leesee, I felt myself becoming close, and I knew I was more of a man than that, so I eased up.

"I don't need my brother to put me up on nothin', especially if he gon' tell me how to do it and what I can and can't do. I'll figure everything out on my own. I'm a man now, I got this." I felt myself becoming more heated than I should have. I was tired of being attacked by them. I felt like it was time for me to stand up for myself.

My mother looked at me from the side of her face and grunted. "Nigga, what you don't have is time. Like I said, you can't stay under my roof if you ain't bringing in no income, and you definitely can't stay if you fucking wit' that li'l girl in any way, shape, form, or fashion. Both of y'all can get the fuck out of my house right the fuck now. I mean it, too." She placed another plate into the dishwasher, mumbling to herself.

"Mama, why you hate me so much, huh? I mean, why do you talk to me the way you do and treat me like I'm not even your child? Even when I go all out of my way to respect you as the queen you are?" I shook my head. "Don't you know you're all I have in this world? That I love you more than I love my own self?" I felt my eyes

108

Love Me Even When It Hurts

stinging, and I was trying my best to not let a tear fall, but looking at my mother for some reason was hurting my soul. I could tell she did not love me one bit, and I didn't understand why. "Tell me, Mama. Please, because I really need to know. I'll leave your house for good and never come back, but you at least gotta tell me somethin'."

She slammed the dishwasher loudly and stood up, looking into my gray eyes. Hers were the same color. Her face read anger and hatred. "Because every time I look at you, I see yo' damn daddy. You look just like his punk-ass, and I hate you for it," she said through clenched teeth.

I frowned. "Then why not hate Kazi, too? You favor him more than me, and he look a hunnit percent like our father. That ain't fair." I blinked and a tear slid down my cheek. I wiped it away immediately. I didn't wanna let my mother see how vulnerable I was over the subject of her love and affection.

She shook her head. "Y'all ain't got the same daddy, fool. I thought you'd know that by now," she scoffed and looked at me as if I was the dumbest person in the world.

Her last comment cut me deep. "What do you mean, we don't have the same father? Then who is my dad?" I asked with my head bowed.

My mother stepped forward and grabbed my shirt into her fist, bringing her face so close to mine her lips were brushing against my own. "The reason that li'l bitch in there sniffing around yo' ass so tough is because she smells Shotgun all over you. Y'all got the same scent. He's yo fucking daddy. I don't know how you didn't put two and two together. He's always throwing that shit in my face every chance he get. That's why I hate yo' ass. That's why I can never love you. Not only is his punk-ass yo' daddy, but he set up Kazi's father to be murdered by his Shotgun posse. All that shit was over me. Once that nigga gets addicted to a female and he misses his meds for a few days, all hell breaks loose, and he goes on these murderous escapades. When he find out you fuckin' that li'l girl in there, he ain't gon' care that you his son. He gon' take yo' life. I promise you that." She let my shirt go and looked me up and down, I guessed to see if what she'd told actually set in.

My head was spinning. Shotgun was *my* father. All these years I'd thought my father was dead when it turns out he was staying right next door. My mind was blown. I really didn't know how to feel or how to break that news to Leesee. I just knew once I told her she'd never wanna mess with me again. I was more sick over that fact than actually finding out about who Shotgun really was.

My mother laughed, nodding her head. "Yeah, that's some truth for yo' ass right there, ain't it? And I ain't done. Let me do you one better. That fool Rah'nell can't even make kids. This whole time Deidre been telling that girl Rah'nell is her real father when I don't believe he is. She was fuckin' wit' him and Shotgun at the same time, so it's a huge possibility Leesee is actually his fucking kid. Or Kade's. She was fuckin' him, too. Found that out the hard way." She lowered her head and shook it. "Deidre always been a ho. At least I was only fuckin' two niggaz. She was fuckin' three. She always been jealous of me, though. That's why I hate hoez."

"Wait, so you saying Kazi's father could be Leesee's dad? Or Shotgun?" I was feeling weak in the knees. I started to imagine what my brother looked like, and in my mind I put him and Leesee's face right next to each other's, searching for similarities. I guess if I had to choose a father for her, I'd rather it be Kade. At least that would free us up to be together.

I was so lost and confused that I didn't know what to do or think. I wished I had never come home. Had I not, I would have never been given this information.

My mother swished her hands together up and down. "I wash my hands of that situation. I don't give a fuck who's daughter she is. Kade is dead and gone. Shotgun killed him, and one day I'm gon' get my revenge. But as of today, you gotta take that li'l bitch as far away from my house as possible. Y'all gotta go right now.

110

Love Me Even When It Hurts

An hour later, I found myself sitting on the edge of a Super 8 motel room bed with my head down. I had so many thoughts going through it that I couldn't think straight. I could not believe Shotgun was my father. I guess it explained why I was so muscular and my brother was so skinny. Also why my hair was naturally curly like his and my brother's was more kinky. I exhaled loudly and rubbed my hands over my face.

Leesee came out of the bathroom with a big, white terrycloth robe on, her long hair flowing curly down her back, stopping between her shoulder blades. She came over and sat right next to me, kissing me on the cheek. "What's the matter, baby? You've been quiet the whole ride here, and ever since you got here. I'll pay a penny for your thoughts," she said, smiling, showcasing the dimples on her cheeks.

Damn, my dimples were just as deep. Shotgun had them, as well as Kade. I was so lost I didn't know what to do or say. "I don't know, Leesee. I guess some of the stuff my mother just said is weighing heavy on my brain. I'm trying my best to not let it affect me, but I'm having a hard time."

She nuzzled her face into my neck and kissed it. "Well, baby, I'm here to listen if you need me to. Or if you just want to sit here in silence, I'll do that, as well. I'll do anything you want me to do because I am so thankful you're in my life right now. All of this shit that's going on with my mother and sister is freaking me out. Now my grandparents aren't answering their phone. I'm assuming the worst, and I need you to help me take my mind off of everything. Can you please do that? Can we heal each other?" she asked, sucking on my neck and nuzzling her cheek against mine.

Even wit' the circumstances looming in front of us, my manhood began to stir. The scent of her went up my nose and left me aroused. I felt my brain becoming cloudy. The need for her rose to an all-time high. I felt her bite into my neck and suck it with force. Now my piece was growing harder and harder, to the point it was sticking out of my waistband. She trailed her hand under my shirt and rubbed my abs, before going lower and crashing into my helmet, squeezing it lightly.

I groaned and threw all caution to the wind. I didn't want to think about any of the things my mother had said. I just wanted to live in the moment. I wanted to be a part of Leesee in every single way. I needed her. Needed to be lost deep within her soul so I could escape the world of pain that was dragging me down, and had been for as long as I could remember.

I lay backward, and she got on top of me, leaning her head down and continuing to suck and bite all over my neck. Every time her teeth made contact with my skin, I shuddered. I took my hands and ran them up and down her back, causing the robe to open up and expose her breasts. She sat all the way up and shimmied her shoulders so the robe fell down around her waist, looking down on me from her dominant position.

"Rome, I'm hurting so bad. I'm so lost right now, and I can tell you are, too. You need me, and this is the only way I'll ever know how to be there for you. So take my body. Use me in any way you need to. I'm yours, I promise." She blinked and tears fell down her cheeks. She wiped them away and proceeded to take the robe all the way off, tossing it to the floor and turning back to me before climbing off of me and standing on the side of the bed.

***

Leesee

I stepped onto the carpet of the motel room, took a step back, and made sure I was standing in front of the lamp. I wanted Rome to see all of me. I needed to see the look in his eyes when he did. I needed him to see me for me, to want me for me, and not for whom I resembled. I took a deep breath and slowly turned in a circle for him with my eyes closed. Idris had made me do this so many

112

times. I always felt so degraded and so weak, and even in that moment I was finding it hard to not break down. I simply wasn't ready for what I knew Rome needed. I was still hurting deep within my soul, broken from years and years of abuse from a man who was supposed to be in my life to protect me.

"Do you like what you see, Rome? Am I still the prettiest girl you've ever seen?" I asked with a lump forming in my throat. Constant flashbacks of nights where Idris made me turn and turn, around and around in a circle for him while he told me how much I looked like my mother when she was my age. He'd tell me again and again how crazy the resemblance made him until he could take it no longer. After all of his restraint was lost, I'd wind up handcuffed to the bed while he did everything imaginable to my body the whole night through.

He sat up and scooted to the edge of the bed, opening his legs and pulling me into them by my waist, reaching upward and brushing my hair out of my face, looking me in my brown eyes with his piercing gray ones. "You super fine, baby. I have never seen anybody on this earth that is half as bad as you. I mean that with everything I am."

He rubbed my tears away with his thumbs, then wiped them on his pant legs, stood up, and kissed my lips passionately, groaning into my mouth. "Mm. Mm. You taste so good, Leesee. But you know we don't have to do nothin' you don't wanna do. I'm cool wit' just being cuddled up with you for the night. I mean that," he said, kissing along my neck, sending chills down my spine.

I nodded. "I know, baby. But do you want me? Do you want me and nobody else? Better yet, who are you seeing right now? I need to know."

I pushed him backward on the bed and straddled his waist again, taking his polo shirt and pulling it over his arms and off his body, exposing that rock-hard physique I had low-key peeped on more than one occasion. This man was so, so fine to me. I couldn't deny that fact. I ran my hands over his chest, then down to his abs, taking pleasure in the muscles there. His penis head throbbed at the top of his waistband angrily. I could tell he was really riled up.

"All I see is you, Leesee. All I've ever saw was you. I need you so bad right now. I swear I do. I'll do anything to have you."

He moaned as I sucked on his chest, taking my tongue and licking his nipples before sucking them. All the while my hands ran all over his abs. More than once I purposely grazed across his helmet just so I could feel his heat. Every time I did, he humped upward into me, closing his eyes tighter as if he were in pain. His scent was intoxicating.

I sucked downward until I was kissing all over his stomach muscles, trying everything I could to focus solely on his pleasure and not the nagging thoughts of whether my mother and sister were okay or the traumatic experiences I'd survived with Idris. I wanted to be there for Rome. I wanted to find a way to lock him down so he would never leave my side, never leave me alone to face the beast of a man that was Idris.

I knew he was coming for me soon. I just didn't know when. What I did know was I was going to need Rome to be there so he could protect me by any means.

"Tell me again, Rome. Tell me all you see is me. Please, I just need you to see me. It's all I ask," I cried, sucking along his waistband.

As my lips wrapped around his big helmet that was sticking up from his pants, he answered me after gasping for breath. "All I see is you, Leesee. You're beautiful, and I will never break away from you. I'll do anything for you. Just tell me what to do and I'll prove it to you."

I pulled his pants and boxers all the way off his legs and pushed them to the floor, grabbed his penis, and stroked it up and down in my hand as the flashbacks of Idris all started to attack me at once, so much so that at first I yanked my hand away from his piece. Then, shaking, I grabbed it again and licked my lips. "I'll do anything for you, too, Rome. Just promise me you'll never leave me. Promise me you'll protect me from Idris, because I'm so scared right now." I started to shake so bad my teeth were chattering.

***

Rome

That was all it took. Once I looked down on her and saw her shaking as if she was sitting naked in a pile of snow, I reached and pulled her up to me, wrapping my arms around her protectively. I wasn't the smartest man in the world, but I had enough common sense to know she was hurting, and she needed me to be there for her on an emotional level. I didn't like seeing her hurting the way she was. I wished I could heal her and take away all of her pain, place her burdens on my shoulders so she could be free of the mental anguish. Though I knew it was abnormal for me to have such strong feelings for her, I couldn't deny I did. I cared about her more than I did my own self.

She started to really shake against me as she broke completely down. "I'm so sorry, Rome," she said with her teeth chattering together. "I really wanna do whatever you need me to do, but I'm just not ready. Please don't be mad at me, because I need you. I don't want you to leave me all alone. I don't have anybody."

She started to shake so bad I got worried. I wrapped her into my arms and placed my leg around her body, holding my body heat against that of her own, trying my best to get her to warm up and calm down. "It's okay, baby. I swear to God it's okay. I don't want you to do anything. It's my job to heal you. I just wanna be here for you so you'll know how much I care." I rubbed her curly hair away from her face and lay my cheek up against her right one.

She continued to sob, but the shaking was slowly starting to subside a little bit. It took ten minutes for it to stop completely. I had to keep on rubbing her shoulder, and kissing her soft cheek in a soothing manner.

Jelissa

After I held her for a while, I guessed she felt strong enough to tell me what was on her mind. I was lying on my back and she was kinda on her side with her head on my chest, rubbing my abs. I think she was fascinated by them, and I was cool wit' that, because I was smitten by her whole body. She was the baddest female I'd ever seen, for real.

She kissed my chest. "Baby, I'm sorry I broke down like that. It's just that I've been through so much in the last couple days. I want with all of my heart to be able to heal you in that physical way you need me to, and I will, but I just have to get stronger. Are you really mad at me? I understand if you are, honest." She looked into my eyes and bit into her thick bottom lip.

I smiled and continued to play with her hair. "I'm good, Leesee. I just wanna make sure you're straight because you matter more to me than I do. I gotta protect you at all costs. Plus I understand you have been through a lot. It's gon' take some time, baby, but it's good. I ain't going nowhere. You ain't gotta worry about that. I promise."

She looked even sadder at hearing those words. "I just don't understand why you care about me so much. We've been living next door to one another for years and we've barely ever talked, but now it seems like we're all we have, and I'm so crazy about you already because I know you're genuine. I don't care how early it is. We connect on a level deeper than time frames. You understand what I'm trying to say, baby?"

I absolutely did. It was crazy how I was feeling her so deeply already, but I didn't want to take too much time to try and break down where we should have been wit' the amount of time we had been rocking together. I just wanted to speed ahead and let this woman know I was crazy about her. I was also having a hard time trying to figure out how I was going to tell her what my mother had told me in regards to Shotgun being my father. I was almost scared to tell her, feared she'd go running for the hills, and I couldn't risk that. I needed her too bad.

Love Me Even When It Hurts

I leaned forward and kissed her soft, pillow lips. "I understand, and I feel the same way. You got my heart, Leesee, and I'm riding for you for life."

She climbed up my body and lay her face in the crux of my neck. I could feel her sniffing me up. "Baby, what do we do about Idris? You know he's never gonna stop coming for us. Aren't you worried in the least bit?"

I shook my head. "Nall. If that fool wanna go to war over you, then it is what it is. I ain't letting him hurt you no more. I gotta make sure of that. I'll die protecting you. That's on my life." I hugged her to me and kissed her forehead. "We gotta get somewhere and settle in so I can get to hustling and get us out of Jersey. We ain't safe here, so I gotta make a way."

She nodded her head, then ran her fingers over my stomach muscles. "I already hollered at my cousin Tia out in Brooklyn. She say we can come stay wit' her for a few months if we need to, or we can rent out the apartment right across from hers. She's the super of her building in Marcy Projects. I mean, I know the space ain't ideal, but at least we'd be able to get the hell out of Jersey for a minute until we can figure out what we're going to do. She lives alone, and she's one hunnit. I trust her, but it's up to you. I just don't want you to leave me." She kissed my chest and lay her face on the spot she'd kissed.

I knew a li'l bit about Brooklyn because some of Kade's people stayed out that way, so I wouldn't be completely unfamiliar. Then, as far as Marcy Projects went, I knew that was a hustling pit. It wouldn't be nothing for me to be able to sell some of those kilos of dope, though I still was unsure as to what they really were, but I intended on finding out real soon. "You know what? I'm wit' it. Call her and tell her we'll be out that way first thing in the morning."

Jelissa

Chapter 12

Shotgun

I fell to my knees and placed my face into the carpet, running my right hand over the spot where my duffle bag should have been, but it was no longer there, and I felt sick to my stomach. I sat back on my haunches and looked down the hallway. I knew for a fact I'd turned that light off before I'd left with Nia and Deidre's bodies. I stood up, shaking my head, the room spinnin' all around me. It'd been four hours since I'd killed William and Martha, leaving their bodies down in their basement inside of their deep freezer. I searched the whole house and could not understand why I could not find Leesee when her voice sounded so clear to me. She had to be close. I was just missing somethin'. I had to be.

I got up and made my way down the hallway, and I could swear I smelled her scent in the air, calling out to me. It made my heart beat faster and faster inside my chest. I missed her so bad. I felt like I was losing myself.

I made my way down the hall and straight into me and Deidre's bedroom, pushing the door, walking to the bed, and tearing the mattress off the box spring, before dropping to my knees, pulling out my small pocket knife, poking a hole right on the side of it and ripping downward. Placing my hand into the hole, I pulled out half a kilo of Peruvian Flake. I sat it down between my legs while sitting Indian-style, opened the package, then brought it up to my nose, snorting it like a maniac.

I felt the cocaine rush directly to my brain before the bells sounded in my head. "Aw!" I hollered. "Aw! Hell yeah! I gotta get my baby back! I gotta get my baby back right now!" I hollered, leaned down and snorted more of the powder into my nostrils.

After getting wired, I stood up with a new prospective. I placed a decent amount of the powder into a Ziploc bag so I could travel with it, stuffed it into my fatigue jacket, and opened my closet door, pulling out another duffle bag that I filled with some of the tools I would need for the next stage of things. It was time to go all out. I knew what I had to do.

Fifteen minutes later I was beating on Shavon's door with a mug on my face. *Whoom, whoom, whoom, whoom, whoom!* The snow had stopped harassing the city, but it was so windy that the force of it was pushing me into her door.

"Who the fuck is it beating on my door like they ain't got no damn sense?" she said, and I could already tell she was pissed off, but I didn't give no fuck. I was on a mission.

"It's me. Open this muthafucking do' before I kick this bitch in. I need to ask you some questions," I said, already losing my temper. Me and Shavon used to fuck around back in day. She was one of the hood chicks who was down with my shotgun posse real tough. A real hood bitch who was 'bout that life. That was until one of my right-hand men by the name of Kade tried to cuff the bitch and turn her into a housewife, not knowing she was a pure ho back then. I found out they were fucking behind my back. Deidre exposed them, which made me and her start to fuck around real tough. Her and Shavon had been best friends at one point, but hoez that fucked around wit' the same crew of niggaz barely ever stayed that way once jealousy set in.

Shavon swung open the door and looked me up and down with disgust. "Nigga, I already know you here looking for that li'l bitch, but she ain't here. I made her and my son get the fuck out of my house a li'l while ago. I don't know where they are or what they're up to, but I told him he's playin' wit' fire, and he don't seem like he give a fuck, so I don't, either." She shuddered as a gust of wind blew into her home.

At hearing that Leesee had been inside her home with her son, I found my blood boiling. I started to imagine him fucking her and doing all kinds of things to her that only I was supposed to do, and I kept on getting madder and madder as each image crossed my mind, especially since I knew the son she was talking about was my own flesh and blood.

I stepped into the house and bumped her out of the way, crushing her freshly-painted toenails with the soles of my Timbs. She reached down and grabbed her toes, hopping up and down on one leg. "Ow, you son of a bitch. I just told you they aren't here. What more do you want from me?" she asked, closing the door behind me.

I ignored her and started to go from room to room, looking for my baby girl. I knew she had to be here. I could feel her presence in the house. "Which one of yo' punk-ass sons was she wit'?" I asked, already knowing the answer to my own question.

"Damn, Shotgun! Yo' nasty-ass Timbs caking mud all over my fuckin' white carpet. Now, I told you that li'l bitch ain't here. She left wit' yo' son a few hours back. Get the fuck out of my house before I call Kazi on yo' stupid ass!" She ran over to me and grabbed my arm aggressively, pulling me toward the front of her house.

I yanked my arm away and pushed her into the wall so hard she made an indent in it. Drywall dust puffed into the air. She cried out in pain. "Bitch, I done already told yo' monkey-ass about putting yo' hands on me. That's what got you fucked up back then, and 'bout to get you fucked up right now," I yelled.

She landed against the wall and closed her eyes, just lying against it in silence. Then she began to shake her head from side to side before she let out a piercing scream. "Argh!" She attacked me with both fists, swinging wildly. "I'm not scared of you, Shotgun. You gon' have to kill me or get the fuck out of my house. You murderer!"

Blow after blow landed against my face, my neck, my chest, and everywhere she aimed for, before I put my guards up and started to block most of that shit.

"Argh!" But she kept on swinging.

I ran away from her just a little bit so I could gather myself. By the time she came again, I was ready. She continued to swing wildly, but I timed her blows, waited for her to throw a left punch. As soon as she did, I jumped backward, then threw a hard left one of my own that caught her square in the chin, knocking her into the wall. She slid down it and wound up on her butt, knocked out cold.

When she awoke, she was duct taped to her chair in her living room, and I was eating a big bowl of Captain Crunch Berries her pantry had provided. She slowly opened her eyes and squinted them at me before they bugged out of her head.

"Rise and shine, bitch. Wake yo' ass up and tell me everything I need to know. And hurry up, because time is of the essence." I laughed, spooning some cereal into my mouth. It felt like I'd not eaten in months, though it had only been two days. My head was pounding and my stomach continued to growl like an angry bear.

Shavon shook her head slowly. "I told you they ain't here, Shotgun. I don't know where that boy took her to. He say he gon' hold her down, no matter what. I ain't got nothin' to do wit' what y'all got going on. Leave me and Kazi out of this. Rome is your son." She sounded like she was out of breath.

I took the bowl of cereal and threw it against the wall. Milk and crunch berries splashed all over the place, even all over my Timbs, but I didn't care. I was pissed off. "Bitch, why the fuck didn't you stop them? Huh?" I asked, grabbed a handful of her hair.

She yelped in pain. "Let me go, Shotgun. You ain't nothin' but a fuckin' bully. I can't stand yo' punk ass. You lucky I ain't a nigga, or else I'da bodied yo' ass, word is bond."

I backhanded her, causing her to shriek in agony. "You would've tried that dumb shit and got left like Kade's soft ass," I said, laughing.

She attempted to stand up, but the duct tape had her well in place. She wasn't going nowhere until I said so. "Bitch-ass nigga. I knew it. I knew you killed my baby daddy, and for what? Why'd you do it, Shotgun? Why?

Love Me Even When It Hurts

'Cause I started fuckin' wit' him and kicked yo' bum-ass to the curb?" she spat with blood coursing from her split lip, down her neck.

For some reason that remark cut me deep. Once upon a time I'd been crazy about Shavon, but after I found out another nigga was hitting her pussy, I just lost all respect for her. She started to make me sick on the stomach every time I saw her anywhere.

I knelt down in front of her with my upper lip curled, placing my hand on her right thigh, squeezing it." Then I laughed, ignoring her as she hollered out in pain. "Shorty, you definitely think way more of yourself than you actually should. What the fuck I look like, killing a nigga over yo' ratchet ass? That pussy ain't even all that good. It wasn't back then, and I know it ain't now, especially since two heads done came out of it," I said, jerking shoulders because I imagined what her shit looked like with her sex lips spread. I just knew that muthafucka had to be wide open cuz both of her boys had big-ass heads, and they had them every since they were newborns.

She groaned in obvious pain. "Get yo' fuckin' hands off of me, Shotgun. You ain't nothin' but a pussy. You making it seem like you all that. Nigga, you ain't shit, either. You can say whatever the fuck you wanna say. I know you was jealous of Kade. You was just mad because he was reaching places in me yo' li'l dick never could, so you took it out on him the bitch way. Then you ain't even have the balls to keep that shit one hunnit. You had to blame it on Rah'nell once he got knocked off, Kade and yo' first partner's murder. You's a dirty nigga, and one day you gon' get yours. Best believe that," she said, looking into my eyes with hatred.

I laughed. "Look, Shavon, on some real shit, I don't give a fuck about Kade, that white muthafucka Ronney, or Rah'nell bitch-ass. It's all about me and my baby girl. She the only muthafucka I care about outside of me, you dig that?"

Jelissa

She sucked her teeth loudly. "And that's another thing, you stupid-ass nigga. Don't you know Rah'nell couldn't even have kids?"

I frowned, and then my eyes got bucked. "What?"

She smiled. "Yeah, nigga, that's right. That nigga been sterile since birth. Everybody knew that except yo' stupid ass. That li'l girl you running around shaking people down for could really be your fucking daughter. You sicko. How that make you feel?" she spat with so much venom I had to stand up.

I paced back and forth in front of her for a few seconds, then put my finger in her face. "Bitch, you bet not be fuckin' wit' me. You trying to tell me Rah'nell ain't her father? That I am?" Even as I heard the question, I couldn't believe what she was getting at. It was blowing my mind on so many levels that I was shaking.

She smirked and nodded. "Yeah, that's exactly what I'm saying. But then again, that bitch Deidre wasn't just fucking Rah'nell on the low. She was fucking Kade, too. The whole time you thought she was just God's gift to mankind, that bitch was going-going. Running like a track star, and you was all up in her ass. Ugh."

My eyes were bucked wide open. I started to hear Leesee screaming my name. Images of her pretty face flashed across my memory's window. It couldn't be true. There was no way. Deidre would have told me, I'm sure of it. I started to shake more and more.

Shavon laughed louder. "Yeah, it ain't no fun when the rabbit got the gun, is it? You run around Jersey all day long fuckin' people over, taking lives just because you see it fit to do so, but when yo' life turn upside down just a little bit, you can't take that shit. Huh, Daddy? Ugh. Nigga could have been fuckin' his own kid for years."

She shook her head, laughing like a maniac while I crawled around the floor on my knees. The reality was too much for me to bear. She had to be fuckin' wit' me. She just had to be.

"You see this shit, Shotgun? You make everybody crazy, just like you. You fucked my head up a long time ago. You took the only man that cared about me away from me. Left me alone, abandoned in this cold-ass world with two little boys. You ripped my heart in two. Now it ain't nothin' that you can do to me." She laughed under her breath, watching me crawl to the wall, placing my back to it before reaching into my pocket for the cocaine. I opened the Ziploc and took a pinch of the contents out, leaning my head backward, snorting heavily. I needed to clear my mind. This could not be my reality.

"Let me go, Shotgun! I gotta pee!" she hollered.

But I was too busy treating my nose to care, hearing my baby girl's voice scream at me. *Kill this bitch, Daddy. Kill her because she's trying to mess with your head. She hates me. She's jealous of us. She told Rome to take me away, and I need you.*

"She long gone by now, Shotgun. All the dope sniffing in the world ain't gon' bring her back, and it's yo' fault!" she laughed with her head tilted backward.

"No!" I made it to my feet, pointing at her. "Bitch, you lying. That can't be true. Deidre would have told me. But you know what? So what if it is? No matter what, she belongs to me, right?"

Shavon frowned. "You're a sick son of a bitch. I knew you wasn't right from the start. You deserve to rot in hell for yo' sick-ass ways."

I rolled up the Ziploc and placed it inside my duffle bag before pulling out the chain from a chainsaw, then the combination lock. I stood behind Shavon. "Bitch, I don't know what you thought this was or what you were doing, but you gon' tell me where my daughter is. You finna call Rome and tell him to bring my baby to me, or I'm finna introduce yo' ass to a Korean necktie," I smiled, Leesee's voice screaming in my head for me to kill Shavon in cold blood.

Shavon moved about nervously in her chair. The duct tape didn't allow her to do much, though. "A Korean necktie? What the fuck is that?" she asked as I placed the chainsaw chain around her neck, flipping it so the blades would be pressed against her skin.

125

Jelissa

"A Korean necktie is this li'l chainsaw blade right here being wrapped around your neck and then locked on with this here combination lock. Once it is in place and set up, you got about an hour to live, depending on how tight I make it." I pulled it backward suddenly, implanting the sharp ridges into her neck.

She gasped and struggled against her bonds. "Shotgun, don't do this. I swear I don't know where they are. The best I can do is call Rome, but what if he don't answer the phone?" she asked with sweating pouring down her forehead. Her eyes were open wide and struggling to look down at the weapon around her neck.

In response, I pulled the chain, causing it to penetrate her. Multiple incisions were made that started to bleed right away. "Bitch, if he don't answer that phone, then you gon' die because it's all yo' fault. You should have never let him leave with my baby girl. This is on you."

As I said that, I heard loud music in front of the house, and then it was silent. Seconds later there was the sound of footsteps on the porch. I took the duct tape that had been sitting on the table, pulled about eight inches off of the roll, and slapped it across Shavon's mouth. I took out my pistol and ran into the living room, ducking down on the side of the door as I heard the key slide into the lock. I cocked back the hammer and waited, holding my breath without even realizing I was doing it until my vision went slightly hazy, then I let out a big gasp of air just as the door slowly opened.

"Mama, where you at? I need to holler at you real quick. And why you ain't answering yo' phone?" Kazi hollered before kicking off his Timbs at the door with his back to me.

By the time he turned around, I was standing up with my pistol pointed directly at him. A big gust of wind blew in from outside, bringing with it a dusting of white snow.

His eyes grew as big as paper plates as he threw his hands up. "Shotgun, what the fuck, man? What you doing in my mama house?"

126

Love Me Even When It Hurts

I grabbed him by his Marc Jacobs leather jacket and put the Glock to his forehead. "Bitch-nigga you betta not move or I'ma put two in yo' head, word is bond." I began searching him for the pistol I knew he had somewhere on him. I knew for a fact Kazi was a young goon. He reminded me a lot of me when I was his age, always wit' a pistol and all about the paper by any means. I think I didn't like him solely for the fact he looked so much like Kade. He was the spitting image of his father.

I located two pistols on him right away, one on his waist, and the other in a holster under his left arm, both .45s. I took them off him and put them on me, then pushed him forward into the living room aggressively. "Get yo' punk ass in there."

He stumbled forward. "Man, what the fuck is this about? Don't nobody be fuckin' wit' you, Shotgun. You on bullshit for no reason."

I pushed him further into the living room, nearly straight into Shavon. When he saw her, his eyes got even bigger. "Mama!" He ran over to her and dropped to his knees in front of her, already starting to take the duct tape away from her mouth. I stood there and allowed him to do that.

As soon as it was removed, she started to sob loudly. "Kazi! Oh, baby, Shotgun done lost his mind, and your brother got us into a bunch of bullshit fucking wit' that li'l girl next door. Do you know where he at?" she whimpered with blood running down her neck.

Kazi wiped her tears away and looked over his shoulder at me. "That's what this shit is all about? Leesee? Man, look how you got my mama, Shotgun. You know I can't honor this shit, nigga." He stood up and mugged me with intense hatred.

I curled my lip and turned the Glock sideways. "Get yo' punk ass back down on yo' knees before I pop you." I dig into my pocket and screwed the silencer onto the barrel of the gun.

Kazi watched me and slowly knelt down, his eyes lowered as if he was thinking about making a move. "This ain't got shit to do wit' us, Shotgun. I kicked that nigga out my trap and told him I wasn't fuckin' wit' him no more after he said him and Leesee were getting down. I know how much you love that li'l girl. I knew this was gon' turn into some bullshit, but that's on him, not on my mother."

I smirked and grunted at that. "Far as I'm concerned, y'all in the same boat 'cause y'all family. The only way I ain't about to kill Shavon right now is if you call that nigga and tell him to bring my daughter to me in the next thirty minutes. That's how long it's gon' take for her to bleed out once I lock this necktie in place." I stood behind her and pulled the chain roughly, making her jerk her head backward.

Kazi jumped up and got ready to rush me when I upped both guns, stopping him in his tracks. He continued to fidget as if he was debating trying his luck, looking from me to Shavon. "You know I can't let you do that, Shotgun. I can't let you hurt my mother no more."

I aimed the silenced Glock at his right knee and pulled the trigger. *Whoom.*

He buckled and dropped down, holding the bloody injury. His blood oozed through his fingers while he cried out in pain. "Aw! Shotgun. You bitch-ass nigga. Ah! I swear I'ma get you for this, cuz. Fuck!" He lay on his back with his right knee pulled to his chest.

I yanked the chain all the way backward, snapping the ridged edges into Shavon's neck. Then I took the combination lock off the table and clicked it in place while she kicked her taped legs up at the air, struggling against the pain so bad she fell to the floor with blood leaking out of her neck profusely.

Kazi started to pull himself over to her. "Mama. Oh my god."

I kicked him in the ass. "Nigga, pull out yo' phone and call Rome. Tell him to bring me my daughter. Hurry up, or yo' mama gon' die. She got thirty minutes. Shavon, the more you struggle, the faster your heartbeat. The faster your heartbeat, the more blood it pushes out of yo' dumb ass, so chill out. You got thirty minutes. Kazi, call Rome, or this bitch gon' die."

Jelissa

Chapter 13

Leesee

"So yeah, girl, y'all can stay here for a few week until you get on your feet. Trust me, I know how it is when you step out on yo' own for the first time. It can be scary, but that's what family is for," Tia said, closing the distance between us and giving me a big hug. She smelled like cocoa butter.

I hugged her tightly and took a step back. I was so thankful for her. Growing up we had always been real close. Whenever I got tired of Jersey, my mother would always let me come out and visit her over the weekend. She was three years older than me and had moved out of my mother's sister's house when she was only sixteen years old. Now at twenty-one, she owned her own beauty salon and was on her way to opening another one. She also worked in a strip club where she swore she brought in no less than five gees a weekend. I didn't understand why she chose to live in the projects, and I never asked her. I was cool with the fact she was willing to help us out for the time being.

I held her hands and looked her in the eye. "Now, can you promise me you won't let anybody in our family know I'm staying here? It's just not safe for me right now, so that's very important. I need to know I can count on you."

She smiled, her brown eyes lighting up, making her dark-skinned, pretty face pop. "I got you, girl. Dang, have I ever given you a reason to not trust me?" She looked into my eyes and jerked her head forward before pulling me into her embrace, hugging me tightly. "I missed you so much. I don't know what all you've been through, but I'm here for you now, and I can see that big-ass nigga behind you is, too. He look like he don't play," she joked seriously.

Jelissa

I broke our embrace and looked over my shoulder at Rome. He was watching us both very closely. "Baby, you okay over there?" I asked, turning around and walking over to him so he could hold me.

As soon as I was close enough, he grabbed me and kissed my lips. "I'm good as long as you are." He rubbed my face, looking me in the eyes.

Every time I looked into those gray beauties they made me feel some type of way. I was so glad he was mine, that he cared about me the way he did, even though I didn't understand it.

Tia walked over to us and stood behind me. "I'm saying if you gon' be staying here, you gotta at least let me know you ain't no killa or nothin'. Give me a hug or somethin'. Let me know it's good. If it's okay wit' you, Leesee?"

Though she was asking me that question, she was looking over my shoulder directly at him as if she were hungry. I knew she was feeling him more than she should have been just off that look alone. It made me a little nervous because Tia was stacked with ass and titties, fine, and had more game than the average chick. She'd been raised in the projects, so she'd always been faster than me on every level. I started feeling insecure, and for the first time I noted she was dressed in some tight, red biker shorts that cupped her ass in the back and her mound in the front. I wondered if Rome had peeped that, and if it was making him feel some type of way. I sure hoped not.

I shrugged my shoulders. "It's good. He can give you a hug. That's harmless." I took a step to the side and she stepped forward and stood in front of him. They locked eyes and I damn near fainted.

Rome looked down at me. "You sure, Leesee?"

She stepped forward again, getting into his face so close their lips brushed one another's. From my vantage point I could see her shorts were all up in her round ass. That made me even more insecure. I did not have a shape like hers, and I wished I had.

Love Me Even When It Hurts

"She said it's cool. Rome, damn. I ain't gon' bite yo' fine ass. We all family up in here."

"Nah, I'm good," he replied curtly.

She took a step back, shaking her head in awe. "Damn, I ain't gon' even lie, this nigga is fine. No disrespect, Leesee, but on everything he can get it. Y'all ain't serious, are y'all?" she asked, looking me over nervously.

I snickered because it was the only thing I felt I could do after being put on the spot like that. "Uh, that's my baby right there, and we figuring things out. It's still kind of early, but we'll see," was my response though I wanted to scream, *bitch, if you touch him I'ma kill yo' ass, family or not. This man means everything to me.*

Tia looked over at Rome. "Mm. Okay, well, I said what I had to say. I guess I'll stay in my lane until y'all ready to carpool wit' me."

Rome grabbed me to him and wrapped me in his big arms with my back to his chest, kissing me on the neck. "This my heart, and even though she ain't there yet, I am. I'm serious as a heart attack about her. Word is bond." He kissed me again. "I wanna hit yo' hand for letting us chill here, too. Huh, here go five hunnit for the rest of the month. You say that li'l apartment across the hall finna open up in three weeks, right?" he asked, digging into his pocket and coming up with a knot of cash. I'd already stepped to the side so he could do him.

Tia nodded. "Yeah, and I'ma make sure y'all get it cuz I'm the Super." She took the five hundred-dollar bills from him and smiled, licking her juicy lips before waving us to follow her to the back of the small apartment. The whole time all I could do was stare at her ass, praying Rome wasn't doing the same thing.

She opened the door to a bedroom that was just across from the bathroom. It was kind of small, but on the plus side, it already had a bed in it so we didn't have to rush out and get one, though I'm sure we would eventually.

"This where y'all gon' be sleeping at. My room right next door, so y'all be gentle wit' each other and try not to wake me up." She laughed and shook her head. "Um, the crib is real small, so I guess we'll have to make do. I really don't have any special rules other than try your best to be courteous and help out with the food. Other than that, it's good. I'm easy breezy."

Rome stepped to the side of me. "Yo, on some realness, I'm trying to hustle a li'l bit, too. Now, I ain't gon' do that out yo' crib, but I do wanna get my feet dirty. I gotta provide for me and her, so I gotta get a move on," he said, walking back into the living room and picking up the duffle bag.

Tia followed him and sat down on the couch, crossing her big thighs. "That's cool. What you fuckin' wit'? Maybe I can get you established with some of the users in the building. I know they been looking for new product, or at least that's what my aunt was saying a couple days ago."

Rome reached into the bag and pulled out a kilo, setting it on her glass table. "Heroin. This shit pure, too. It ain't been stepped on or nothin'. Anybody mess wit' me, they gon' get more than they bargained for. I'ma make sure of that."

Tia nodded and licked her lips. "Damn, and you got money, too. Leesee, where you find this nigga at? He seem like he the total package." She scrunched her nose. "Mm! Let me make some phone calls, and I'ma put you in wit' my homegirl's baby daddy. They stay one floor down. He one hunnit, real stand-up. He just got fucked over on trying to cop some work from some niggaz out of the Bronx, so he gon' be all over this."

Fifteen minutes later Rome was in the living room hollering at some dude named Pappy, and they seemed like they were hitting it off. I noticed Rome was watching him real close and asking a lot of questions about the projects. Questions that all revolved around hustling.

Meanwhile, I was in the room pacing back and forth, trying to gain my sanity. Neither my mother nor my sister had returned any of my phone calls, and I was starting to freak out. Idris, on the other hand, had blown me up, calling me over eighty times and leaving me about half as

Love Me Even When It Hurts

many text messages I refused to read. I didn't even want him to know I was still alive. A part of me wanted to read them just to see if there would be any mention of my mother and sister, but I knew better so I didn't.

I exhaled loudly and continued to pace. My situation was causing me to have a heavy heart. I needed to see my father, and I was thinking about going out that way this weekend. I just needed to be in his presence. I needed him to hug and hold me and tell me everything was going to be alright, even though he couldn't know for sure.

Rome came into the room and closed the door behind him, walked over to me, and pulled me to him before wrapping his big arms around me possessively. "Baby, you okay in here? I ain't mean to be out there so long. I'm just trying to see what this hustle game in Marcy finna be like 'cause I gotta make sure you eat and keep the best of everything. I don't want you needing or wanting for nothin'. I got this. You hear me?" he said, looking down on me with a serious look.

I smiled and nodded. "I already know, baby. I believe in you, and I know you got me. I just want you to be careful and know you don't have to do all of this for me. I am perfectly fine with you just being by my side. Your protection is everything to me." I hugged him as tight as I could and felt his phone buzz, but he ignored it.

"You're everything, Leesee. I need you to love me, man, because I ain't never had that from nobody before. I don't know how I'm going to make it happen for you, I just know I am. I can't see myself failing you. I need to put my life on the line for you just so I can have a reason to live, because for so long I wasn't finding one. If you only knew what I been through in life, it'd blow yo' freaking mind, baby. I swear." He held me tighter. "I just wanna be loved. That's all I ask."

I lay my head on his chest, listening to his heartbeat. "Baby, I watched them beat you on so many occasions in that backyard. I watched you get up covered in your own blood on so many nights that I wanted to call the police. So many times I cried about what they did to you because

135

Jelissa

I don't understand it. How could a mother allow those things to happen to her child? How could a brother beat his brother senseless and force him to sleep in the cold, unprotected from the storm? You didn't deserve any of it, baby. I wish I could have saved you from it all," I whimpered as I felt the tears fall down my cheeks. The memories of his assaults replayed over in my mind. The punches, the smacks, and all of his blood decorated the snow after they were finished with him.

I took a step back, stood on my tippy-toes, and kissed his lips. "I do love you. I'm falling harder for you every minute we are together. Every time I learn more about the man that stands before me, willing to put his life on the line just to protect me, I love you that much more."

He took a deep breath and blinked tears. "Just give me a chance to earn your love, Leesee. Give me a chance to prove to you I am everything you'll ever need. I'll forever love and protect you with all that I am."

His phone buzzed again, and this time he pulled it out of his pocket and looked at the face. His eyes moved back and forth as he read the text that appeared across the screen. "Aw, shit! This Kazi. I'm finna put him on speakerphone because this message can't be real."

Seconds later I could hear his brother's voice on the phone.

"Rome? Nigga, is that you?" he asked, sounding winded.

"Yeah, it's me. What's good wit' this message you just sent me, bro? I thought we wasn't messing wit' each other no more," he said with a frown on his face. "Now you hollering 'get at you cuz it's an emergency'? What emergency is that?"

"Bitch-ass nigga, this muthafucka got our mother snatched the fuck up because of you. I can't do too much talking on this phone, but I'm fucked up right now. I need you to bring that bitch to the crib or our mother gon' die. Trust me when I tell you that. This ain't a fuckin' game, either."

Love Me Even When It Hurts

Rome looked over to me and we locked eyes. He shook his head. "Look, bro, I done told you about disrespecting her. That shit ain't cool. You don't even know her like that to be callin' her out of her name."

"Nigga, I don't give no fuck about that bitch! That ho finna get our mother killed if you don't bring her ass home. Now quit playin' Captain Save-A-Ho and get her the fuck here. If I lose my mother over you playing these muthafuckin' games, word is bond, I'ma have every Crip nigga on the east coast at ya dome, bruh. This nigga Shotgun going on a rampage over his punk-ass daughter. Got my mama tied up and shit. Now– Uh! Uh! Uh!"

"You doing too muthafuckin' much, snitch-nigga!"

The phone was quiet for a few seconds. I could hear a bunch of rustling, and then Idris came onto the line. "Hello? Hello, Rome?"

Once again me and Rome locked eyes. "Yeah, this me. What's good?" He was now starting to pace the small expanse of floor.

Idris cleared his throat. "Look, Rome, all I want is for you to bring my daughter to me and we can stop all this bullshit. She need her father, and I need my baby girl. I don't know what's going on, but all these games gotta stop."

Just hearing his voice caused me to get weak in the knees with fear. I fell down to a sitting position, shaking like a leaf. I was praying Rome wasn't about to turn on me. The things Kazi said Idris had done to their mother sounded pretty severe. I wondered if he'd trade me in for her.

Rome attempted to hand me the phone, but I pushed his hand away and shook my head. I was terrified.

"Look, Shotgun, she ain't rocking wit' you like that no more. She wit' me now, and ain't shit moving. All that bull you done to her ain't happening no more. Go on wit' yo' life."

"You li'l bitch-ass nigga. You don't know who you fuckin' wit'! I'll kill you over my baby. Fuck you mean she wit' you now? She ain't never gon' leave her daddy.

Jelissa

Bring me my baby or I swear to God you gon' regret it. You hear this shit?" I could hear what sounded like someone gurgling on water. It was loud and clear. "Nigga, that's yo' mama, and she sitting her dying because of yo' sins. I'ma let this bitch drop the fuck dead, too. Then, instead of me killing yo' brother, I'ma release him so he can get at yo' ass. Now, is all that worth a female, huh?" he asked, and in the background I could still hear the gurgling sound.

Once again me and Rome locked eyes. He looked worried. "Look, man, you on this bullshit." He exhaled and looked toward the ceiling, still holding the phone to his mouth.

"Wait, baby, let me talk to him," I said, standing on wobble legs. He handed me the phone and stood to the side, rubbin' my back real supportive-like. "Hello, Idris?" I said, barely above a whisper. I was so scared I felt like I was about to throw up. I don't know what was going on with me.

"Baby. Oh my god. Hey there, baby girl. How are you doing?" he asked, all sweet and fake.

I started to shake so bad Rome had to hold me up. "I'm okay, but I'm not ever coming back home. You need to let me go on with my life, Idris. What we had wasn't right, and you know it. I just want to start over and go a different route, so please allow me to do that," I whimpered with tears streaming down my face. My chest began to heave up and down faster.

The phone was silent on the other end, and then Idris snapped out, "What the fuck you mean you ain't never coming home? I need you, and I need you right now. Ain't nobody gon' keep me away from my baby girl, not even you. I told you a long time ago, Leesee, that you belong to me. Now get your ass home before I find you and take you off this Earth, please." His voice started to crack up. It sounded like he was getting ready to cry.

"Leave me alone. You are my mother's man. Love her and not me. Please. You have to let me live my life. I'm tired of this."

138

Love Me Even When It Hurts

"Fuck Deidre! That bitch is dead, and she could never be you. You are mine, and you're so perfect. I need you, Leesee. Can't you see that?"

Now I could tell he was crying as plain as day, but that wasn't what got my attention. "What did you just say about my mother being dead?" I asked, falling to my knees and imagining the worst.

"You never have to worry about her again, baby. She'll never hurt you or try to keep us apart, I promise."

I dropped the phone, and Rome reached over me and picked it up. "You a sick muthafucka, Shotgun. I don't give a fuck what you do to them, but you gon' stay away from Leesee. Have a nice life." He ended the call, then lowered it to me so I could see he had it on record the whole time. "I recorded all that shit he said, so one way or another he gon' get his. That fool sick." He knelt down and wrapped me in his arms again, holding me. "It's okay, baby. I'm right here. I got you, and I ain't going nowhere. You got my word on that."

I kept imagining Idris doing all sorts of things to my mother. I wondered if he was the reason for my sister missing, as well. I was so lost. I knew he was coming for me. He'd do the unthinkable to me, and I felt bad because I was pullin' Rome and his family down right along with me. "Rome, I need you to come somewhere with me."

He continued to rub my back, rocking me from side to side as if I were a little kid. "Where is that, baby?"

I exhaled loudly. "I need you to ride out to see my father with me. I haven't seen him in a while, and I just really need to be in his presence right now."

Rome held me tighter. "I'll go wherever you need me to go. Just tell me when you wanna leave."

Jelissa

Chapter 14

Shotgun

I dropped the phone to the floor and fell to my knees. They had gotten into my baby girl's head and turned her against me. My head started to spin and my vision went blurry, turning a shade of red.

"Shotgun, come on, man. My mama over there dying. Take that thing off her neck. She ain't got nothin' to do wit' this. Put it around mine. I'll take her place," Kazi said, crawling on his stomach toward Shavon.

I hopped to my feet and mugged the fuck out of him. "You think I care about this bitch, li'l nigga? Huh?" I grabbed the padlock and pulled it backward to make the ridges go deeper into her neck. She started to jerk in the chair, kicking her legs as blood poured from her wounds onto her chest. "Y'all taking my baby girl away from me. Turning her against me. Making her think I'm the enemy!" I pulled backward, but this time she was no longer fighting against me. She sat perfectly still, but it didn't stop me from pulling more and more.

Kazi sat up and tried his best to make it to his feet. "Nall, Shotgun, you killing her. You killin' my mutha-fuckin' mama for no reason," he cried and hopped over to her.

I took my pistol and slammed it into the side of his face, cracking him open. He flew into the wall and slid down it with his eyes wide open. "This ain't on me. It's on yo' brother. He did this shit. He kilt Shavon, not me." I knelt down and put my pistol in his face, pressing it so hard into his forehead it broke the skin. "Listen to me, nigga. If you go to them people on me, I'm gon' make sure this shit get switched up and be placed all on you. You want street justice, that's one thing, but going to the law'll get you fucked over, my nigga, word is bond."

Kazi took four deep breaths in a row and clenched his teeth. "Nigga, I'd never go to you bitch-ass police about

141

Jelissa

shit. I'm killing Rome, then I'm coming for you, Shotgun. Word is bond, we gon' handle this shit in the streets like men, cuz." Tears fell down his cheeks.

I thought about killing him right then and there, but that would have been too easy. I knew with him also hunting for Rome and Leesee I'd find them faster. I could always come back and finish him later. In my eyes he wasn't even a challenge.

I grabbed him by the throat and placed my face as close to his as I could without actually touching him. "You gon' get yo' chance, and when you do, you better make yo' first move yo' best move. I'ma handle you just like I handled yo' punk-ass father." I pushed him backward and stood up, looking over Shavon's dead body. "Clean this bitch up. She's bleeding."

On my way out of the house I started to make a few phone calls to my crew, calls I should have made a long time ago because it was time to get down and dirty and reclaim my old self. The first thing I had to do was finish the job with Deidre and Nia's body. After I took care of that, I went to William and Martha's house, wrapped their bodies up, and followed the same procedure I'd enacted with Deidre and Nia, burned their bodies in the big, metal garbage can for a few hours, then pulled out the bones and beating them into dust before burying them in the woods.

After that was concluded, I ran Leesee's license plate and reported her truck stolen. Then I drove to my house and waited for Hunter to show up.

***

Rome

Leesee climbed into the bed and snuggled against me, lying her head on my chest. "Baby, are you coming out so you can put some food on your stomach? I made cheeseburgers and homemade French fries. I need you to eat something because I'm starting to worry about you," she said, rubbing my stomach.

142

Love Me Even When It Hurts

Food was the last thing on my mind. I was too busy trying to get over the screenshot of my mother Kazi had sent me less than a hour ago. She was in a chair with some sort of device around her neck, obviously deceased. My mind couldn't process it fully without wanting to shatter. "Baby, I'm not hungry right now. Not since Kazi sent me this." I held up the phone so she could see the screenshot of my mother's dead body. I still couldn't believe Shotgun had went to those lengths. I felt like it was my fault she had been targeted. Now Kazi was talking about killing me on sight and having every Crip out east come at mine and Leesee's heads. I was almost afraid to tell her that part, though I knew I had to.

She took the phone out of my hand and put her left hand to her mouth in awe. "Oh my God, Rome, I'm so sorry. I don't know why he would have done somethin' like this. He is supposed to be a police officer. Are you okay? Is there anything I can do for you right now?" she asked, handing the phone back to me. She started to rub my chest.

I exhaled loudly and shook my head. "I know it's my fault, but to be honest I don't know how to feel. I mean, it was either you or her, and I will never let that fool hurt you again. I loved my mother with all of my heart, but I know for a fact she didn't care about me one bit. She only loved Kazi, and it's been that way ever since I could remember."

I tried my best to sit all the way up. She sat back so I could make that move. Once my back was against the headboard, I sighed and prepared myself for the worst, which would be losing her after I told her everything I was getting ready to. I had to keep it all one hunnit with her, especially since I knew from then on out it would be us against the world. "Leesee, I got some things I need to tell you, and I don't want you to interrupt me. You have to let me finish, and then we can face it all together. Do you understand me?" I asked, getting out of the bed and looking down into her pretty face.

143

Jelissa

She nodded and bit into her bottom lip. I could tell she was nervous. "Okay."

"Before all of this happened, my mother told me there is a strong possibility Shotgun is my father. In fact, she was almost sure of it. She said it was the reason she had basically hated me my whole life." I lowered my head in shame.

Leesee slapped her hand to her mouth and sat up straight on the bed. Her eyes were wide open, and she looked as if she were in shock.

I didn't know whether I should have moved forward or left it at that, but I pressed on. Everything had to come out. Our life had to start anew that night.

I looked at her for a long time without saying a word until she gave me the rotating hand signal for me to keep going. "Well, that's not the only thing she told me. She also said Rah'nell, your father, is sterile, and has been ever since some car accident he had when he was a kid. She said there is no way he could be your father." I said the last part so low I didn't think she heard me.

She jumped out of the bed and removed her hand from her mouth, shaking her head in disbelief. "No, no, that can't be true. He's the only father I've ever known. If not him, then who can it be? Did she tell you that?"

Before I could answer her question, there was a knock at the bedroom door, then Tia stuck her head in the room. "Hey, I need to use your Jeep to run to Wal-Mart. I get my car out of the shop tomorrow. Is that cool?" she asked, puffing on a blunt with her eyes already super low.

Leesee walked over to the dresser, got the keys, and handed them to her. "Go ahead, but don't be driving all crazy and shit. I can tell you're high as hell."

Tia laughed. "Yeah, that's why I ain't finna do no driving. I'ma let Pappy do that." She stepped back into the hallway and closed the door.

As soon as she was gone, Leesee turned back to me and looked me up and down. "Well, did she tell you who it could really be, if it's not Rah'nell? Because all of this is blowing my mind in the worst way." She sat back down, looking up at me.

Once again I took a deep breath and blew it out loudly. "She said it's either Kade, Kazi's father, or Shotgun."

I couldn't even bring myself to look at her right away. All I heard was her gasp loudly, then she fell to the carpet on her knees, crying her little eyes out. I dropped down to console her as best as I could.

"No, no, no, Rome. That can't be true. You have no idea what I've done with this man. It has to be Rah'nell. It just has to be." She cried louder, and then as if somethin' hit her, she stopped and jerked her head backward, looking up at me with eyes wide open. "Wait a minute. If your mother is saying Idris is really your father and there is a potential he's mine as well, what does that mean for us? Oh my God, is that the reason you're telling me all of this?" She looked as if she was becoming hysterical.

I shook my head. "Nah, Leesee, you bugging. I just wanted to let you know everything. I don't want to keep nothin' from you because you deserve the truth." I tried to pull her into my embrace, but she knocked my hands away.

"You're going to leave me, Rome. You see what Idris has done to your mother, and now you regret your decision to stand by me like you said you would. Just fuckin' leave, then." She fell to her knees and broke all the way down.

I fell down beside her and put my arms around her, hugging her tightly with tears in my eyes. I didn't know what our truth was or what we were about to be up against, taking on both Shotgun and Kazi. But I did know I wasn't going to leave her side. "Baby, listen to me. I am here with you for the rest of my life. I love you, and I will never turn my back on you. Now is not the time for us to turn on each other or lose sight of what we're up against, because things are about to get really real."

She lay her head on my chest and continued to cry. "But I just love you so much, and I don't want you to ever leave me, no matter what our truth is. I don't even wanna know. All I need is you, Rome. You're all I care about."

I shook my head. "Never, baby. I swear on my word as a man, I will never leave you. We are in this together, until my last breath." I exhaled, and my tears became more fluid. I couldn't stop them from falling. I started to imagine my mother's face and the last sight of her with the device around her bloody neck. I hated that she'd never loved me, and I also hated the fact it was going to come down to me and my brother having an all-out war. I knew he was deeply plugged in with the Crips, and Capo, their chief, gave him a lot of headway. His word was golden. All it meant was at every turn I had to watch mine and Leesee's back, because I knew without a shadow of a doubt Kazi was coming, and he was going to come hard.

"Baby, there is one more thing I have to tell you, and then we gotta get out of here. We need to put a little more distance between ourselves and Jersey."

Leesee picked her head up and looked me over closely. "You can tell me anything, baby, just as long as you aren't telling me you're going to leave my side. I can't take that," she whimpered, then sniffed her snot back into her nose.

I wiped her tears away and shook my head. "I already told you that will never happen. But listen, Kazi coming for us, and the only reason I'm a li'l worried is because he got them Crip niggaz under his command all over the east coast. If he gave them the order for our murders, we're good as gone. Trust me when I tell you this. So we gotta get a move on and put some distance between us and Jersey. I ain't feeling like Brooklyn is far enough. That nigga's hand reaches at least this far."

Leesee looked like she was worried out of her mind. "So, that's Idris and him? What do we do? Where do we go?" she asked with her entire body shaking as if she was freezing.

I didn't have those answered just yet. All I knew was we had to figure things out, and we had to figure them out real fast because our time was running out.

Love Me Even When It Hurts

We stayed in the room for the next hour in silence. I didn't know what to say. My mind was spinning like a top, and I was pretty sure hers was, as well. We had both found out a lot of things that were potentially life altering, and due to our circumstances we didn't know if we would be able to handle the real truth of them all.

Leesee wrapped her thigh around my waist and stuck her face deeper into the crux of my neck. "Rome, do you think your love for me will ever change? I know you're saying it won't, but what if your mother is right about Idris? Then what?"

I didn't know how to answer that question, and to be quite honest, I didn't want to think about it too much. I just wanted to focus on our survival and get the hell out of New York. We needed to go someplace safe where I could love her in the way she needed me to. I didn't want our potential realities to be the death of the relationship we were starting to build.

Before I could let her know what was on my mind, I heard the front door open, and then the sound of screaming. I jumped out of the bed and slid my hand under the pillow, pullin' out the .40 Glock just as Tia busted into the room with blood covering her shirt.

"They killed him! Oh my god, Leesee, they killed him and Janice," she wailed at the top of her lungs.

Leesee jumped up and looked like she was about to pass out. "Who the hell are you talking about?" she asked, grabbing Tia by her shoulders.

Tia yanked her shoulders away and dropped to the floor. "Pappy. They just shot up your Jeep and killed him and Janice right in the parking lot downstairs. They didn't have to do them like that. Now what is her kids going to do?" she cried.

I felt sorry for whoever the hell Janice was and her kids, but the number one thing on my mind was getting Leesee to safety. We had to get out of that building, and fast. I could only imagine the only reason they'd gunned down the pair in the Jeep was because they thought it was me and Leesee.

147

Jelissa

There was a loud beating on Tia's door. It sounded like somebody was trying to knock it down. She jerked up and wiped away her tears while I picked up the duffle bag and put it on my shoulder.

"Come on, Leesee. Let's get the fuck out of here."

Tia jumped up. "Wait, where y'all going?" she cried, looking from Leesee back to me.

The banging started again, this time louder than before. Now both girls were shaking and scared out of their minds.

"Tia, do you got a back way up out of here?"

She nodded. "Yeah, but it only leads to another part of the hallway. Why do you ask me that?"

Leesee threw her coat on as the banging at the front of the house started to sound like kicks. Somebody was trying to knock the door down.

"Let's get out of here, Rome, please!" she yelled, pulling my arm toward the back of the apartment.

Tia shook her head. "Y'all gotta take me wit' y'all. They probably thinking I had something to do wit' Pappy getting shot up, but I swear I didn't. I don't get down like that no more."

"Tia where is this door?" I hollered. The kicks were getting louder and louder. I could have sworn I heard a bunch of male voices. I wondered who it was. Was it Shotgun's boys who had tracked us down, or was it Kazi's Crip niggaz?

Tia led us to a door located inside of her pantry. We rushed inside of it, and I damn near broke my neck unlocking it and pushing it in. As soon as the door swung in, it seemed like a million rats rushed into her house. Big, red-eyed, screeching-ass rats with sharp teeth.

"Ah! What the fuck?" Leesee screamed, jumping and wrapping her legs around me as I kicked them out of the way five at a time.

We were going through the door with Tia leading the way just as the gunshots sounded behind us, and then it sounded like Tia's front door was kicked in. I softly closed the door we had come through and continued to

148

Love Me Even When It Hurts

follow Tia through the narrow space that led back out to the hallway.

We must've brushed past a million rats before we were back on solid ground. As we made it to the hallway, there were about ten dudes who rushed in the direction of her apartment a little way from where we were. We were able to see them because we had not fully come out of the narrow space her pantry had led us into.

As soon as they passed, I placed Leesee down and we made a dash for the stairwell.

Jelissa

Chapter 15

Shotgun

"That's two hundred thousand dollars in cash and five hunnit gees in Fentanyl right there. I'm giving you this, Capo, as payment for the life of Kazi's li'l brother, Rome, and for the life of the girl he's with. Her name is Leesee. I want them both taken out, and the sooner the better, because I can't think straight as long as they are alive. Also, in exchange for their lives, I'll make the indictments on a few of your boys go away. Don't ask me how, just know it'll happen. You have my word on that," I said before leaning down and tooting up a healthy line of Peruvian flake. I was tired of missing Leesee and imaging Rome's punk ass between her thighs. The only way I was going to be able to go on with my life was if she no longer had breath in her body. I was turning her over to the streets, and I knew for certain Capo would make sure the contract was properly fulfilled.

Capo sat back in his chair with two big-ass pit bulls on each side of him. Both were snow white with pink noses and had heads the size of a grown man. He picked up the bottle of Patron, and took a long sip from it before grunting, "Why should I trust you, Shotgun? Everybody know you a dirty muthafucka. You been fucking over my niggaz ever since you turnt pig. Yo' money ain't no good here." He snapped his fingers and two big, bald-headed niggaz appeared, looking like body builders on steroids. "Kid, get this pig out of my trap before I fuck around and catch a case on his snake-ass," Capo said with the right side of his lip curled up.

Before his two big-ass wrestlers could apprehend me, I held up my hand. "Hold on, Capo. I'll leave without a fight, but it's somethin' I wanna let you know." I lowered my eyes into slits and mugged him with hatred, then pulled out my phone and brought up the live feed Hunter

Jelissa

was supplying me with. Then I turned the screen around so he could see it.

He leaned forward, looked closely, and then his eyes bugged out of his head. He reached under his chair and pulled out a .40 caliber and aimed it at me. "You bitch-ass nigga." He stood up and cocked the gun. "I'ma kill you!"

I slammed my forehead to his barrel. "Nigga, go ahead, and both of them li'l bitchez dead. You think I give a fuck about yo' kids, huh? You don't care about mine." I grabbed his gun and held it steady. "Do it, nigga. Come on. I ain't got shit to live for, anyway, so you might as well."

One of his bodyguards took a step back and looked on in amazement. "This nigga crazy. Capo, this fool done lost his mind. He must be doped up on that shit."

"Kill me, muthafucka, or fill that contract! Now, which is it going to be?"

***

Leesee

It was hell getting out of Marcy Projects because it seemed at every turn there was a group of dudes looking for us, though we weren't even sure if they were or not. I was so scared I could barely breathe. I was so thankful Rome was there to protect me and keep me from harm, and so was Tia.

Somehow we managed to make our way out of the back of the building and into the night while all of the commotion was going on in front. We ran for blocks and blocks until we caught up with a city bus and climbed aboard, all three of us huffing and puffing as if we had asthma.

Shortly thereafter we checked into the Ramada Inn, where Rome said we needed to regroup and gather ourselves. He was pretty sure we were under attack, and a few nasty text messages from Kazi confirmed we were. I didn't know where we were gonna go next, but as long as

152

Love Me Even When It Hurts

Rome was beside me, I knew we'd be okay, even with the odds stacked up against us.

All of the secrets he'd revealed to me were messing with my head, and I really needed to get clarity from the only person I knew would never lie to me about anything.

I took a deep breath and stood up in the visiting room as Rah'nell, the only father I had ever known, made his way over to me with a smile on his handsome face. As soon as he got close enough, he hugged me and kissed me on the cheek. "Baby, what a surprise! What brings you here?"

I took a step back and looked him over as the waterworks started to come full blast. "I need for you to tell me the truth about everything. Are you my father? And if not, please tell me who is."

***

Rome

I sat there in the parking lot with so many things running through my head it was hard to concentrate. I didn't know which of our enemies had tried to gun us down in front of the projects, and as crazy as it was to say, it really didn't matter. It didn't matter because all it did was tell me the war was on and them niggaz was playing for keeps. I had to do everything in my power to protect Leesee and myself. I'd rather die before I let her be harmed. I had to get my weight up. I had to get my bearings in the game and place myself in a strong position so I could make it all happen for us. It wasn't going to be easy, but I loved her, and I was willing to do anything for my baby until my last breath.

I hit the latch on my seat and let it all the way back with my head on the headrest. I was tired out of my mind and had not gotten any sleep in nearly three days. My eyes were now trying to close on their own to force me into slumber. I shut them and took a deep breath. Leesee's visit with Rah'nell would last for at least two hours. I was sure

153

she was going to learn the answers to all of our questions. Answers that could make or break us.

A part of me feared the worst, and then there was a part of me that felt like we were unbreakable. I needed to rest my mind for at least an hour. Then I was sure I'd be a lot better. I didn't know what our next move was going to be, or what we'd do wit' Tia, but I was certain I'd figure it out.

I couldn't have been sleeping for more than thirty minutes when I heard the sound of tires screeching on the asphalt and cars slamming on their brakes. My eyes popped open just in time to see the masked men jumping out of the two vans that had pulled up alongside the Navigator I'd rented. They were heavily armed. They surrounded the truck, and I dropped to the floor of the driver's seat and covered my head as the shots erupted in rapid fashion.

To Be Continued...
Love Me Even When It Hurts 2
Coming Soon

Thank you for taking the time to read my book and giving me a chance to showcase my creativity. I hope you enjoyed this story. I appreciate all the love and support.

Mental Health and Wellness is *not* a game. It *should not* be taken lightly. You never know what mental battle a "normal person" may be fighting. It shouldn't take the death of a loved one to comprehend how serious Mental Health is. I, too, struggle with a mental illness. Check on your friends and family. Sometimes an "I'm okay" may be a cry for help.

Thanks again for giving me a chance. I'm new out here in these streets of the literary world, LOL.

Please stay connected with me. Add me on Facebook at Authoress Jelissa Shanté/Author Jelissa Shanté as I have two pages, and please feel free to join the Feenin' For Fiction Readers Group, as well as the Mental Health Matters Support Family Group. God bless.

Love Always,

Jelissa Shanté
AUTHORESS

Jelissa

Submission Guideline

Submit the first three chapters of your completed manuscript to ldpsubmissions@gmail.com, subject line: Your book's title. The manuscript must be in a .doc file and sent as an attachment. Document should be in Times New Roman, double spaced and in size 12 font. Also, provide your synopsis and full contact information. If sending multiple submissions, they must each be in a separate email.

Have a story but no way to send it electronically? You can still submit to LDP/Ca$h Presents. Send in the first three chapters, written or typed, of your completed manuscript to:

LDP: Submissions Dept
Po Box 870494
Mesquite, Tx 75187

DO NOT send original manuscript. Must be a duplicate.

Provide your synopsis and a cover letter containing your full contact information.

Thanks for considering LDP and Ca$h Presents.

BOW DOWN TO MY GANGSTA
By **Ca$h**
TORN BETWEEN TWO
By **Coffee**
BLOOD STAINS OF A SHOTTA **III**
By **Jamaica**
STEADY MOBBIN II
By **Marcellus Allen**
BLOOD OF A BOSS **V**
By **Askari**
LOYAL TO THE GAME **IV**
By **T.J. & Jelissa**
A DOPEBOY'S PRAYER **II**
By **Eddie "Wolf" Lee**
IF LOVING YOU IS WRONG... **III**
LOVE ME EVEN WHEN IT HURTS
By **Jelissa**
TRUE SAVAGE **V**
By **Chris Green**
BLAST FOR ME **III**
By **Ghost**
ADDICTIED TO THE DRAMA **III**
By **Jamila Mathis**
LIPSTICK KILLAH **III**
CRIME OF PASSION **II**
By **Mimi**

Jelissa
WHAT BAD BITCHES DO **III**

KILL ZONE

By **Aryanna**

THE COST OF LOYALTY **II**

By **Kweli**

SHE FELL IN LOVE WITH A REAL ONE **II**

By **Tamara Butler**

LOVE SHOULDN'T HURT **III**

RENEGADE BOYS **II**

By **Meesha**

CORRUPTED BY A GANGSTA **III**

By **Destiny Skai**

A GANGSTER'S CODE III

By **J-Blunt**

KING OF NEW YORK III

By **T.J. Edwards**

CUM FOR ME **IV**

By **Ca$h & Company**

GORILLAS IN THE BAY

De'Kari

THE STREETS ARE CALLING

Duquie Wilson

KINGPIN KILLAZ II

Hood Rich

<u>Available Now</u>
<u>RESTRAINING ORDER **I & II**</u>

By **CA$H & Coffee**

Love Me Even When It Hurts
LOVE KNOWS NO BOUNDARIES **I II & III**

By **Coffee**

RAISED AS A GOON I, II, III & IV

BRED BY THE SLUMS I, II, III

BLAST FOR ME I & II

ROTTEN TO THE CORE I III

By **Ghost**

LAY IT DOWN **I & II**

LAST OF A DYING BREED

BLOOD STAINS OF A SHOTTA I & II

By **Jamaica**

LOYAL TO THE GAME

LOYAL TO THE GAME II

LOYAL TO THE GAME III

By **TJ & Jelissa**

BLOODY COMMAS I & II

SKI MASK CARTEL I II & III

KING OF NEW YORK I II

By **T.J. Edwards**

IF LOVING HIM IS WRONG…I & II

By **Jelissa**

WHEN THE STREETS CLAP BACK I & II III

By **Jibril Williams**

A DISTINGUISHED THUG STOLE MY HEART I II & III

LOVE SHOULDN'T HURT I II

RENEGADE BOYS

By **Meesha**

A GANGSTER'S CODE I & II

By **J-Blunt**

159

Jelissa

PUSH IT TO THE LIMIT

By **Bre' Hayes**

BLOOD OF A BOSS **I, II, III & IV**

By **Askari**

THE STREETS BLEED MURDER **I, II & III**

THE HEART OF A GANGSTA I II& III

By **Jerry Jackson**

CUM FOR ME

CUM FOR ME 2

CUM FOR ME 3

An **LDP Erotica Collaboration**

BRIDE OF A HUSTLA **I II & II**

THE FETTI GIRLS **I, II& III**

CORRUPTED BY A GANGSTA I & II

By **Destiny Skai**

WHEN A GOOD GIRL GOES BAD

By **Adrienne**

A GANGSTER'S REVENGE **I II III & IV**

THE BOSS MAN'S DAUGHTERS

THE BOSS MAN'S DAUGHTERS II

THE BOSSMAN'S DAUGHTERS III

THE BOSSMAN'S DAUGHTERS IV

THE BOSS MAN'S DAUGHTERS **V**

A SAVAGE LOVE **I & II**

BAE BELONGS TO ME

A HUSTLER'S DECEIT I, II

WHAT BAD BITCHES DO I, II

By **Aryanna**

A KINGPIN'S AMBITON

160

Love Me Even When It Hurts

Jelissa

BROOKLYN HUSTLAZ

By **Boogsy Morina**

BROOKLYN ON LOCK I & II

By **Sonovia**

GANGSTA CITY

By **Teddy Duke**

A DRUG KING AND HIS DIAMOND I & II III

A DOPEMAN'S RICHES

By Nicole Goosby

TRAPHOUSE KING **I II & III**

KINGPIN KILLAZ

By **Hood Rich**

LIPSTICK KILLAH **I, II**

CRIME OF PASSION

By **Mimi**

STEADY MOBBN'

By **Marcellus Allen**

WHO SHOT YA **I, II**

Renta

Love Me Even When It Hurts

BOOKS BY LDP'S CEO, CA$H

TRUST IN NO MAN

TRUST IN NO MAN 2

TRUST IN NO MAN 3

BONDED BY BLOOD

SHORTY GOT A THUG

THUGS CRY

THUGS CRY 2

THUGS CRY 3

TRUST NO BITCH

TRUST NO BITCH 2

TRUST NO BITCH 3

TIL MY CASKET DROPS

RESTRAINING ORDER

RESTRAINING ORDER 2

IN LOVE WITH A CONVICT

Coming Soon

BONDED BY BLOOD 2

BOW DOWN TO MY GANGSTA

Jelissa

Made in the USA
Middletown, DE
31 March 2021